Love at the Pickleback

Cocktails For You

Susanne Matthews

i

PUBLISHER

MHSLM

COVER ART

Melinda De Ross

ISBN: 9798345874080

Book Description

How far will Andie go to pursue her dreams?
Determined to marry only for love, Andie leaves the
family's cattle, horse, and oil empire to remake
herself as a bartender at an LA Comedy Club. LJ,
the new owner's go-to man, a man with secrets, can
resist temptation, but not the enticing bartender.
When the truth comes out, will their love be strong
enough to keep them together?

Andressa Myers is determined to live life on her
own terms. Being an heiress to a multibillion dollar
fortune is one thing, but having to marry one of the
men her father considers the best bulls for his littlest
heifer is another. She wants to be loved for herself,
not Daddy's billions. After suffering through a
disastrous twenty-fifth birthday party where she
meets four out of the five men her father has
selected for her, she's more determined than ever to
find a husband on her own. Convincing her father to
let her travel for a year is no small feat, but with her

half-sisters help and a good old-fashioned hissy fit, she manages it.

But Andie has no desire to travel. She wants to experience real life, and LA seems to be the perfect place to do it. All she needs is a job. After a few cosmetic alterations to her appearance, and a slight change to her name, Andie Harper gets hired as a bartender at an LA Comedy Club. With time running out and her search for Mr. Right seeming to have fizzled, she has to make a choice: go home and give up on love or beg Daddy to give her more time.

Things go from bad to worse when she learns the club's been sold to Rayburn Enterprises. The fifth suitor who failed to attend her party is none other than Cole Rayburn, the company's new CEO, a man every bit as elusive as the legendary Howard Hughes.

Fearing discovery, Andie's concerns fade away when she recognizes the bar's new manager. L J Simons, the man who worked as a waiter at her birthday party, is kind, considerate, movie-star gorgeous, but doesn't recognize her. Sleeping with the boss is never a good idea, but she soon finds herself head over heels in love. Their relationship sizzles, and she's certain that this is the man she'll marry until, on the night of the club's grand reopening, a woman with a mouth the size of Texas recognizes her.

Will discovering her true identity destroy her relationship with LJ? But not all the secrets are revealed, and when that happens, will Andie stay or run   away?

Praise for Other Books in this Series

Enjoyable easy, breezy read. I laughed aloud more than once, learned about some alcoholic beverages, and had a nice escape from everyday life following Savannah on her journey to New York. Luke was just the "cherry" on top! (Make Mine a Manhattan)

I loved this Cocktails for You novel, as much as I did every story from this series. When there's an initial dislike between the hero and heroine, the romance is even sweeter as it finally unfolds after a lot of funny banter and flying sparks. Awesome story! (Emerald Glow)

When Zak and Marissa are brought back together, they know there's only one for them, they're a perfect match. Highly recommend for romance lovers everywhere! Susanne Matthews writes the best second-chance stories ever. (It's a Match)

CONTENTS

I wasn't looking for love; I was looking for freedom. Imagine my surprise at finding both with you.

Anonymous

CHAPTER ONE

Tonight should've been a joyous occasion. Instead, it came second only to the way I'd felt when my mother had died. Today marked my loss of what little independence I had and of any chance to live the life I wanted with the man I loved by my side.

"Happy twenty-fifth birthday, Andressa," I intoned, staring at the reflection in the mirror, a made-up doll I scarcely recognized. "Life as you know it ends now ... well maybe not immediately, but as soon as you walk down those stairs, the clock starts ticking. It sucks!"

My voice echoed in the empty bedroom. Sighing heavily, feeling like a condemned prisoner putting the rope around my own neck, I fastened the sapphire and diamond necklace my father had given me earlier today to commemorate the occasion, my Myers Coming of Age Day, the milestone I'd dreaded for the last ten years. Sure, I could access a whole lot of money without anyone's permission, but there was a catch … there was always a catch.

I raised a hand, its artificial sapphire fingernails covering my own, and touched the beautiful rope of stones she'd loved and worn more often than any of her other jewelry. He'd gifted it to her the day I'd been born, claiming that the blue stones, my birthstones, matched her eyes.

After her death, he'd set it aside for me along with the matching earrings. As a bonus, he'd had a coordinating tennis bracelet made that was large enough to be worn around my ankle or used as a collar for my newest step-mother's poodle, Cecily.

Gee, thanks, Daddy. I'm not quite that fat.

Tonight, I would wear it and try to keep it from falling into anyone's drink. Tomorrow, I would take the oversized bauble to the jeweler to be resized and

have a cocktail ring made with the extra stones—
not that I usually wore rings or attended many
parties. I was far too introverted for that, and the
thought of making small talk with all the rich and
famous members of Daddy's social circle who
gossiped about his unattractive youngest daughter,
was intimidating. They would be polite, comment
on how lovely I looked, and bus my cheeks with air
kisses before retreating to their chosen lairs and
ripping me apart. Was I exaggerating? Maybe, but I
was self-conscious about my appearance and hated
being the center of attention.

I consoled myself with the thought that as bad
as I expected things to be, much of the interest
would be on Becki and Cecily. No doubt many of
those present were there to gawk at my father's
latest trophy wife and her pampered pet, the only
designer-gowned dog in all of West Texas. Seeing
the spoiled, little beastie trot around in her doggy
diapers and finery always caused a kerfuffle
wherever they went. Children probably expected the

circus to be in town and were no doubt disappointed when they saw Becki instead.

The members of the immediate family—three half-sisters, their husbands, four step-mothers, their most recent spouses, and my seven young nieces, aged six to twenty, thanks to the failed attempts at providing a grandson—had also been invited to celebrate the fact that I was now front and center in the Myers Marriage Sweepstakes. Unfortunately, only the men my father found suitable were able to purchase a ticket.

I could still hear his vile words from earlier. Just the thought of them made me cringe.

"Happy Birthday, Andressa. Your future husband will be quite pleased with you and your abilities. If any of my daughters will provide me with a grandson, it's you. If only your mother could see you now."

If only she could.

"Mama, how I wish you were here."

She would know how to get me out of this. Mama had been able to wrap Daddy around her little finger, a skill I'd yet to acquire. Truth be told, as much as I admired and respected the man, there were times when his single-minded determination scared the daylights out of me.

Future husband? A man I didn't know? Didn't love? A man who was buying me for whatever bargain-basement price my father was offering, in an effort to secure a grandson for his empire? Was it any wonder that I wasn't thrilled with the idea?

Staring at my primped and polished image in the full-length mirror, I huffed out a breath. Was it so wrong to want a little of that physical beauty to be real—well, as real as it could be? Was it really sinful to want to be attractive and have men pursuing me, men I could vet for myself and decide whether or not we had a future together? It seemed my father thought so.

Growing up, I hadn't considered my looks, or rather my lack of them, to be a big deal. I wasn't beautiful like my older half-sisters, but I wasn't homely … I had great cheek bones. To be honest, I'd never been a girly-girl, constantly worrying about makeup and clothes. If someone made an unkind comment about my height, weight, or appearance, I learned to laugh it off, cloaking myself in Mama's loving words.

"Andressa, physical beauty is fleeting, at the mercy of time and nature. You've got a beautiful soul and a generous heart. Someday, someone will see that just as I do."

Unfortunately, after her death and my exile, at a time when I needed love and compassion, each of those nasty comments became a knife wound to my ego and self-esteem. Rich, pampered, teenage girls were among the nastiest vipers in the universe.

As an adult, working with the horses Mama had loved, I'd considered myself beyond the pain of being less than beautiful. I wasn't, and today an army consisting of a cosmetician, hair designer, manicurist, pedicurist, and dresser, had brought each and every flaw to the surface, if you could call being a throwback to ancestors long dead a shortcoming. They'd done their best to turn the ugly duckling into a swan, but it was all smoke and mirrors or rather cosmetics and undergarments.

My eyes, hair color, and skin so fair that it burned in the shade were traits inherited from Mama's Scandinavian grandparents, but I was far from the beauty my Brazilian-born mother had been, having inherited the worst traits of both her maternal family and Daddy's ... nose too large for my face, droopy eyelids, myopia, the weak chin my father hid behind a beard, and worst of all, no boobs—or as Daddy would say, two cackleberries, both yolks busted. Being flat chested or having hypoplastic breasts had been an asset when I'd dreamed of being an Olympic swimmer, but reality and my asthma had put an end to those fantasies before my twelfth birthday. Unfortunately, by twenty-five, I'd expected a little growth.

Other than my fairness, I resembled my father, and while that might've worked for him since most of his wives had admired his wallet and stock portfolio rather than his physique, it wouldn't work for me. Women, especially those in my father's social circle, were expected to be tall, slim, beautiful, and busty.

A few months ago, I'd run into a woman I'd always considered a friend since neither of us were the epitome of magazine-cover beauty. She'd had a nose job to repair a deviated septum. In truth, it was a relatively small change, but she looked 100 percent better, and the change was obvious in the way she held herself and the confidence she exuded. When I'd returned to the ranch, I'd mentioned cosmetic surgery to my father in the hopes that it would improve my appearance. Just getting rid of the glasses would be a step in the right direction.

That had gone over like a lead balloon and had resulted in a lecture on the sin of vanity and disrespecting God's gift.

What gift? It was a matter of genetics, and I'd drawn the short straw. All of my half-sisters had gotten their looks from their mothers, Daddy only contributing the X-chromosome to their genes. Unfortunately, I'd had no say in his generous donation of centuries of Myers DNA. I would gladly have done without his Roman nose, weak chin, and lack of height. While I couldn't blame him for the droopy eyes and myopia, gifts from the Scandinavian side of the family, no ancestor seemed responsible for my flat chest.

The twins, Alison and Aileen, twenty-one years my senior, were tall and slender, despite each having given birth to three daughters, and had their mother's chestnut-brown hair and hazel eyes. I was darn sure Aunt Raylene did something to keep time and Mother Nature at bay since she hardly looked like a seventy-year-old grandmother.

Amalia, only fifteen years older than me, had inherited her athletic mother's olive complexion, deep brown eyes, and naturally curly black-brown hair. At sixty, Aunt Sophia unwrinkled and hair without a single silver tress, was still involved in running her second husband's business, an exclusive travel agency that specialized in unique adventures for all the adrenalin junkies out there. Amalia, the mother of a thirteen-year old girl, was slightly shorter and heavier than the twins, but had breasts I'd envied for as long as I could recall.

Added to the previously mentioned failings, not only was I plump, with an innate craving for carbs, but I was also short, barely five feet tall, which meant the extra twenty pounds I struggled to lose were obvious. It wasn't as if I sat around gobbling bonbons all day, but I was short waisted and while the underwear that was barely a step above a torture device could keep everything tucked inside for tonight, nothing could disguise the thunder thighs and muffin top forever.

Since Dad had no problem improving his lot in life by increasing his fortune, not caring who might suffer in the process, I failed to see how a nose job, chin and eye lifts, breast implants, and laser surgery were sinful. He'd had no problem with the braces I'd worn for years to straighten my teeth. Why was this any different? If God gave one the means to do better, weren't we obligated to do just that?

How many times had I heard him say, *The Lord helps those who help themselves*? That was all I wanted to do. I was well aware of my limitations. I might not be able to get any taller than the Norwegian troll I resembled, but being more attractive was bound to add to my self-confidence and improve my life. I might even find a way to cut back on my beloved foods and ditch those twenty pounds. In the words of Wayne Gretzky, a hockey player I admired, *you missed 100 percent of the shots you didn't take.* I had to take my shot soon because I was on borrowed time.

Reluctantly, I slipped my feet into four-inch heels, knowing that by the end of this dog and pony show, they and my back would ache. It wasn't that I didn't dress up. I did every Sunday when I went to church, and each evening for dinner—when Daddy was home. At any other time, I considered primping to be a waste of time and effort.

As a rule, I spent my days at the stables working with the wranglers rather than at the Myers Building in Lubbock. Remote working was more than acceptable, especially since the pandemic, but how could I run a breeding stable without being near my horses? Mama had taken a hands-on approach, and so did I. I took my responsibilities seriously, and instead of power suits, I walked around the ranch in comfortable jeans, baggy t-shirts, and custom made leather boots that gave me a lift without inflicting pain.

Should I call tonight by its rightful name? It wasn't a birthday party. Using one of Daddy's favorite analogies, this was a cattle auction with the prize heifer paraded before the buyers, each one hand-picked by my father, one of which would end up with me as the grand—or should I say booby—prize. Would I have a say in the matter? Not likely. When Daddy made a decision, nothing could get him to change it—nothing but Mama, and she'd been gone ten years.

Blowing out a heavy breath that ruffled my lips in an imitation of a frustrated Carmen, my favorite riding mare, I applied the lipstick the cosmetician had left for me. The makeover had been a gift from Amalia, perhaps not one that I'd wanted or enjoyed, but I knew she had my best interests at heart. More like a second mother than a sister, she was well aware of what Daddy had planned for tonight, having lived through it herself fifteen years ago. She was the only one who saw the real me ... the scared, lonely girl who still mourned the loss of her mother and hid behind a façade of indifference, jokes, and sarcasm.

As much as I hated to admit it, the makeup had improved my looks, but who had time to learn how to primp and contour? Doing so for at least an hour each morning would be a complete waste of time. Would the horses care? Besides, all this gunk on my face would probably leave my sensitive skin red and blotchy. No. I needed a permanent solution that didn't involve war paint, contact lenses that thanks to my droopy eyelids bothered me, armored underwear, and falsies.

Reaching for the bottle of perfume my best friend Ingrid had sent me, I applied it sparingly. The floral aroma was light, unlike my current step-mother's musky scent that I found overpowering, but at the moment, the beautiful Becki ... with an *i* not a *y* ... only three years older than me, could do no wrong. She'd married my seventy-five-year-old father for his money, and he'd wed her for her family's steel mills. Their pre-nup, like all the others he and his brides had signed, looked more like a business partnership, complete with an exit clause, rather than an offer of marriage. Like his previous two alliances, there would be no son from this marriage. I was his last child, his last heifer as he put it, a run-in with prostate cancer having rendered him sterile twenty years ago, hence his insatiable need for a male heir.

Glancing in the mirror once more, I cringed.

While the lace gown was exquisite, dressed all in white as I was, my long hair intricately woven and plaited, hanging down my back, my lips deep coral, my cheeks rosy thanks to the overuse of blush, and my carefully made up eyes filled with fear, I resembled the one thing I dreaded more than anything else—a bride—and a sacrificial one at that. At the moment, the idea of being tossed into a volcano to appease the gods, or tied to rope pillars and left on a cliffside as an offering to the Kraken was actually more appealing than attending my own birthday party.

Why? Because *they* would be there, the suitors my father had handpicked for me, the men desperate enough for money that they'd marry the ugly half-sister to get it.

According to the twins, women I admired but had never been close to given our age difference, the mix of desperate men included a dethroned prince who considered himself a king, the aging playboy son of one of Daddy's longtime business associates, a rancher from Montana who was running for Congress, and the great-grandnephew of a former US president. The fifth menu selection and the one Alison deemed the frontrunner was Cole Rayburn, heir apparent to Rayburn International, a corporation with its fingers in more pies than even my father had. To the best of my knowledge, Quaternity, my father's company, and Rayburn Enterprises weren't in business together, the latter being involved in restaurants, hotels, casinos, nightclubs, and other entertainment venues.

Efficient, informed, and just plain nosy, I'd searched the Internet for information on all of his choices, far from impressed with the social footprints I'd found, but what I'd learned about Cole Rayburn had been dang sparse. There were a few photographs of him with his parents, but unless Daddy was planning to marry me off to a fourteen-year-old baseball player with a wicked batting average, none of those images were current. According to what I'd read, his parents had been killed when their small plane was struck by lightning, and he'd been raised by his mother's family in Massachusetts.

The adult male, now twenty years older, was a recluse, which to my way of thinking meant there had to be something wrong with a multimillionaire who didn't want publicity. Heck, Daddy made a point of being on the cover of some dang magazine or newspaper both the hard copy kind and the ones online, every month. So why didn't this Cole?

Had he been aboard the plane with his parents? The sole survivor of that horrific tragedy? Was he physically deformed because of it? Emotionally stunted after such a traumatic event? From what I could see, he'd quit playing sports and had withdrawn from the human race. There was no mention of education, post-secondary or otherwise, but the man had to be smart enough since the plan was to have him step into the company's top position. So why would he be willing to saddle himself with me if it wasn't simply because his company needed an infusion of Myers money? Could it be because he wanted a brood mare to carry on the family name and wouldn't be able to get one the old-fashioned way? Neither option appealed.

My father, whose own matrimonial record was rather dismal, might have decided that as family patriarch it was up to him to select the best possible mates for his daughters, marriages based on common interests and business and financial goals that would last, but I disagreed. Marriage should be more than a business transaction, designed to improve the company's bottom line.

It was true that my half-sisters were content with their lots in life, seemingly in love with their husbands who were similarly enthralled with them. Arranged marriages were nothing new—they'd been around for centuries, although on this side of the world they were rare. Quaternity and my father had gained from each arrangement as had the men, since each union had come with a lucrative job and a title as a signing bonus, and while my father doted on his seven granddaughters, he still wanted a grandson.

Anderson, Alison's husband was Daddy's second-in-command and oversaw the oil side of things. Richard, Aileen's husband, was the company's financial head, and Dan, Amalia's husband, looked after the legal side of things. The family business consisted of the largest cattle ranch in West Texas, a thoroughbred stable, which I currently managed, one of the country's most productive oil fields, an up and coming vineyard in

Southern California, as well as several other financial moneymakers my father had acquired through shrewd negotiations or one of his marriages, most of them run by trusted men who knew what they were doing and made the family richer one minute at a time. When he passed on, my sisters and I would each inherit one fourth of Quaternity. He believed only he could choose the right men to maintain the solvency of the company, and since he'd done so well with the first three, he was satisfied with his ability to pick winners.

If and when I married, I wanted more from wedlock than a pre-nup, a new employee on the books, and a line in the plus column of the company's accounting software. I wanted love. Was that so much to ask? I had no intention of emulating my step-mothers and sisters, being nothing more than a decoration on my husband's arm, raising children from a distance, sitting on the boards of the various charities and foundations they espoused, or attending tea parties and hobnobbing with the rich and famous, essentially having no self-identity. I wanted my marriage to be a loving partnership where my spouse would support me just as I did him.

Even the Crown had allowed the younger generation to choose their own mates. It was time someone dragged Daddy, kicking and screaming, into the twenty-first century. Women had rights. They were allowed to own property, work, vote, and make their own damn decisions about the things that affected their lives.

Queen Elizabeth II had married for love, and while duty might've come first, her marriage had stood the test of time, whereas Daddy was on wife number six. Mama had been number three, the only one so far who'd died rather than divorcing him and reaping the benefit of the handsome settlement set out in their pre-nup. After Mama, there had been Charlotte and Desiree, but I scarcely knew them, since neither had stuck around for more than a few years each, and I'd spent most of that time away at school. Who knew how long Becki would last? It wasn't as if she'd married for love ... none of them had, not even Mama, although she'd come to love him deeply over the seventeen years they'd had together, the longest lasting of any of his marriages.

Forcing myself back to the present, I patted the sophisticated basketweave cap of hair on the top of my head, surprised to see that the curls on each side of my face hadn't wilted yet. I hadn't been able to prevent my sister's hairdresser from snipping off those two locks to allow her to frame my face, but there had to be something I could do to stop what I knew would happen tonight. Daddy would choose one of his pet monkeys, and my life, my independence as I knew it, would be over.

"Grow a backbone, Andressa. You know what you want; go for it," I demanded of my mirror image, but while she repeated my words, she had no advice to give me.

I stomped away from the mirror almost twisting an ankle in the process.

I was smart. Surely, given my skills at rationalizing, I could come up with some kind of argument to convince my father that given time and a chance to be anonymous, I could find a man of my own, a man who would love me for me, not my father's wealth and influence. I hadn't asked to be born with a whole damn silverware set in my mouth, and I refused to let that fact destroy whatever chance I had at happiness.

Was I being naïve? Maybe. Money, especially a lot of it, changed people. It had changed Ingrid's father, and when the girls at school had realized who and what I was, it had changed them, too. Once my mystery man discovered who I was, it was possible the dollar signs would fill his eyes, cloud his vision, and he'd become just like all the other rich men I knew, somewhat selfish and condescending. But my life and happiness were at stake. People learned more from failure than success. If I failed, then so be it. I would do it Daddy's way, marry one of the insufferable men he selected for me, and become the Texan equivalent of a Stepford wife, but if I succeeded, what a wonderful life I could have.

Glancing at my watch, I sighed. I had fifteen minutes before I was expected to meet the photographer in the study down the hall for my official birthday portrait, one he would air brush to his heart's content. After that, I would walk down the staircase and greet the guests. Since my mother couldn't be here, I'd asked Amalia, my favorite half-sister, to walk down with me. Daddy would be too busy watching his choices, working the room, and interacting with his ex-wives, something that might prove entertaining.

A good old-fashioned cat fight might spice things up, but since this was a family occasion with a lot of important people and the press present, every one of them would be on her best behavior. Having five step-mothers present wasn't that unusual in a crowd that married and divorced as often as most people changed their cars—my friend Ingrid had seven, one for every day of the week. Besides, I was too big a coward and a klutz to risk going down the stairs alone, taking a header, and further humiliating myself.

I'd been dreading this day for years, ever since I'd realized that all three of my sisters had been married off shortly after their twenty-fifth birthday. Alison had been first. I'd been four and dressed in enough bubblegum pink tulle to resemble a chubby little cupcake as I'd preceded my half-sisters down the aisle. Six months later, attired this time in buttercup peau de soie, we'd repeated the action for Aileen. At the time, I'd been in awe of my half-sisters, both beautiful brides in designer dresses the cost of which could probably have fed small countries. Alison had cried her way down the aisle, while Aileen had been more composed. Six years later, gowned in a seafoam chiffon dress befitting a Junior Bridesmaid, I'd followed my niece Laura, Alison's five-year-old daughter, down the aisle ahead of the twins and several of Amalia's closest friends, as the last of my sisters got married.

I sighed. If I'd learned anything after Mama's death, it was that once a Myers girl turned twenty-five, Daddy's ambitions took over, and her future was his to dictate. For all the control I now had over my fate, I might as well have been born during the Middle Ages.

The sound of someone knocking on the door pulled me out of my memories.

"Come in."

Amalia stepped into the room, teetering on heels that had to be six inches high, making her appear six feet tall. The most attractive of my half-sisters looked amazing. She'd pulled her shoulder-length, curly, dark hair away from her face to highlight the diamond earrings her husband had given her for her fortieth birthday. The low-cut, peacock blue, silk dress accentuated her bust and the diamond teardrop pendant she'd added to the neckline. It fit her like a second skin, whereas my high-necked dress hung loosely, hiding all of my body's imperfections, the sapphires around my neck, wrist, and in my ears, the eyeshadow I wore, and the deep blue nail polish providing the only pop of color.

She smiled and came over to me.

"Andressa, you look lovely," she oozed. "I know you weren't excited about my gift, but having your makeup and hair done for tonight was the right thing to do. You have no reason to play the shrinking violet now. Go out there and wow them with your sense of humor. You're every bit as lovely as I knew you could be, as Aunt Anya, your mother knew you could be. I know you don't believe me, but honestly, your appearance isn't as dismal as you think. All Mel did was do what she does best, bring out your natural beauty."

I chuckled. "Natural beauty? I doubt that, but she definitely knows how to turn a sow's ear into a silk purse."

My sister shook her head. "You're far too hard on yourself. You're really quite pretty; it's just that you don't put any effort into your appearance. Daddy insisted you wear white tonight—we all had to—and while I tried to convince him otherwise, given your coloring, he stuck to his guns. A brighter colored dress would've been better, but Mel did a fantastic job. You look amazing." She raised her hand. "I'm not saying you should do it every day, although my mother, outdoor adventure queen that she is, still made a point of teaching me that a woman needs to be at her best all the times, no matter what she may be doing. Your mother felt the same way, but dying at that critical stage in your life, and then Daddy forcing you to spend your teen years in that dreary school … The twins and I should've done more to help you."

I shook my head. "There really wasn't anything the three of you could've done. You were adults with responsibilities, and I'd just turned fifteen. It was hard at first, but once I met Ingrid who was pretty much up the river in the same leaky boat that I was, it wasn't so bad. She's happy now, married to a man she adores that she met when she started nursing. I want what she has, Amalia. I want it with every fiber of my being, and I can't imagine not fighting for it. If Mama were here, she would agree with me. I may not have appreciated being sent away so soon after her death, but it was probably for the best. Daddy threw himself into work, and

Charlotte came on the scene." I sneered at the thought of the woman who'd replaced my mother in his bed, even if her sojourn there had been a relatively short one.

Amalia nodded, the sympathy in her eyes hard to miss.

"Not his finest hour, I agree."

"He didn't know how to deal with a hormonal, grieving teenager, and I couldn't handle a new step-mother with mine gone less than a year." I chuckled. "By the time any of you were my age, you hadn't been living here full-time. I'll admit it was probably guilt, not love, that let him give me more freedom over the years. Look at the way he's let me take over the stables." I swallowed the concern clamoring to be released. "I wish he was still filled with that guilt, but it seems my birthday capped that well." I snorted. "I don't suppose you have any advice that would help me get out of going down there tonight? I considered taking Ipecac syrup, but he'd probably just drag them all up here to admire me as I puked the night away."

She laughed. "Would you really want to miss your own birthday party, or do you simply want to avoid meeting the men Daddy's selected for you?"

"Both," I admitted. "Avoiding those men is a given, but you know how uncomfortable I am around people, especially in crowds."

She stood and paced the room, turning suddenly to stare at me, her forehead creased.

"You're wrong, Andie."

CHAPTER TWO

Tears threatened. No one had used the pet name my mother had given me in years. I swallowed the lump in my throat and blinked to keep the sudden tears at bay. Normally, I was cool and collected, logical to a fault, but tonight … I was an emotional mess and that probably wouldn't improve.

"I've seen you fraternizing with the wranglers, the salesmen, the farm hands, the servants, and even the city slickers who come here to watch the bronco-busters or rent a horse for a few hours. You've held your own and excelled at horse auctions and rodeos. Your best friend didn't come from money although her surgeon husband has done well for himself. Being around people in general isn't your issue, it's being with the wealthy ones in our family's social circle. Why? You're every bit a part of this group as they are."

"Am I?" I cocked my head. "While they were all getting to know one another, going to cotillions and coming of age parties, I was in the boonies where Daddy didn't need to worry about me, and then later instead of coming back to Texas for university, he sent me to Cornell for Veterinary Studies, although he won't let me practice anywhere but here. I've been back on the ranch barely a year. It's a miracle he let me take complete control of the stables. The people I'm comfortable with don't expect anything from me. They've come to know me, and well, they don't judge me the way the high and mighty do. They've seen me mucking out stalls, delivering breeched calves, and making my own bed."

"I love you, dearly," Amalia retorted, "But I think Anderson's right. You've become a reverse snob, maybe not a bleeding heart liberal as he claims, but you're darn close."

I threw my hands up into the air.

"Seriously? How can you say that?"

My cheeks didn't need the blusher to be red now as indignation overtook fear. When I'd tried to convince Daddy last evening that this marriage auction wasn't necessary, Anderson had taken my father's side, claiming I was too young and inexperienced to make such a critical decision. Jerk! If I were a man, I'd feed him a knuckle sandwich.

I glared at my sister. Here I thought she'd agreed with me. Obviously, I was mistaken. Jumping to my feet, almost tripping over the rug beside the bed, and rounded on Amalia.

"How can you take his side now, especially after what he said last night at dinner? Too young to know my own mind? Alison may think Anderson is the best thing since John Deere invented the plow, but while he's an excellent businessman, he's far too focused on the company's bottom line. He claims to want to run for office, but he would be there for the glory and honor it brought him, not for the good of the people he represented. There are times when he opens his mouth and spouts those God awful lies and that idiotic party line. He doesn't have the balls to go against them, so what makes him think I've got the same rubber spine? I may avoid confrontation, but, when push comes to shove, I can stand on my own two feet. I'd like to see him standing at the hind end of an elephant waiting to deliver."

I was all worked up now, thoughts of what I would like to do and say to my supercilious asshole brother-in-law erasing my fear.

Amalia smirked. "You do paint a pretty picture. Don't hold back. You're magnificent when you're all riled up. I recall your Mama telling Daddy that one day, you would have enough of being the obedient child and when that day came, you'd throw a conniption the likes of which he'd never seen. There are times I admit when Anderson goes too far and insinuating himself in this situation might be one of them, but he's really no worse than any other politician. They can campaign making all kinds of promises, but once they're elected, it's all about towing the party line."

I sighed, all of my indignation whooshing out of me like the air in a leaky balloon.

"I just think someone should worry about the ordinary people instead of their own bottom lines. Dad certainly doesn't."

"Doesn't he?" She came close to me once more, her eyes filled with sorrow. "Think about that for a minute. Does anyone working here in the house, on the cattle ranch, in the stables, or on the oil rigs look miserable to you? Don't they all get paid vacation, health insurance, meals while they work, housing as needed, and regular hours? There are no slaves here, Andressa. The family has always worked side by side with the help. I suppose you don't remember Daddy doing it, but he did for years, as did the rest of us. I looked after the stables after Anya died or did you forget that? I may not have done it inside with the horses as you do, but the thoroughbred breeding turned a profit back then, too. You're simply more hands-on than the rest of us."

Subdued by her words, I nodded. I was inclined not to give Daddy and Anderson the benefit of the doubt.

"You're right, but when it comes right down to it, having happy employees benefits Daddy in the long run. I don't see him or Anderson clamoring for the fair treatment of others down on their luck."

Amalia sighed. "Honey, you've got a lot to learn about life. Anderson's right about one thing. You *are* naïve. You've been sheltered, kept away from as much of the ugliness as possible. Didn't you ever wonder why Daddy chose that place for you after your mother died? He knew you'd be safe and sheltered there, out of the eye of the paparazzi. There's no such thing as an issue with only two sides. There are all kinds of exceptions and nuances. Before you start tar and feathering Daddy and Anderson, you need to look a little deeper. They aren't perfect, no one is. As my husband likes to say, 'Only one perfect man walked this earth more than two thousand years ago, and look what they did to him.' In his own unusual way, Daddy does love us all and has our best interests at heart."

I huffed out my frustration. "Dan's probably right, but a nice, small, quiet celebration with only the family would've been in my best interest," I grumbled.

"Sorry, but no Myers girl comes of marrying age without a gala. If your Mama had been alive, there would probably be twice as many people here. She loved a good party. Daddy's throwing this shindig tonight for you and tossing Becki to the wolves to take off some of the pressure. You didn't think of that, did you?"

I shook my head. I'd assumed she'd hijacked the party I didn't really want for her own purposes.

"He knows you don't like being the center of attention, and in his mind, he's trying to make it easier for you by pitching her into the ring. The funny part is I don't think she even realizes that she's nothing more than cannon fodder. In his own way, he loved your mother more than any of his wives. Maybe that's why he's dead set against the surgery you want so desperately. If I can see her in your eyes, so can he, and once you get rid of the Myers' traits … it'll probably be like seeing the woman he loved and lost. Now, as to the Matrimonial Stakes, it really won't be as bad as you think."

"How can having no say in the choice of the man I marry be good on any level?"

She narrowed her eyes and shook her head.

"Where did you ever get the idea that you have no say? Alison, Aileen, and I all had a say. Why would you think you wouldn't have one? You were young, it's true, but we all made an informed choice. I got to know Dan and spend time with him before I agreed to marry him. All Daddy is doing is sifting through the chaff and bringing you the best choices—like handing you the chef's selection in a restaurant. Nothing but the best, right? It made it easier for me to find the man I love—and I do love him. We've had fifteen years together, and God willing, we'll have many more. Has it all been sunshine and roses? No, and losing the baby, the son we both wanted and discovering I couldn't have another, took a toll on us, but any marriage worth having is worth fighting for."

I huffed out a breath. "You make it sound so logical, but what if I don't like any of the men he offers me tonight?"

She fixed her gaze on me.

"You deserve to be loved and happy, Andressa, and while you may not believe it, it's what Daddy wants, too. This may make tonight easier on you. Cole Rayburn, Daddy's number one draft pick as Alison puts it, won't be here and has sent his apologies. His great-grandfather had a bad fall and is in the hospital. Instead of flying here from wherever he was, he has to go to New York. Since he's next in line for the company throne, he has to look after things until the elderly man recovers. Leland Rayburn retired ten years ago but came back to run the company when his son, Carlton, Cole's uncle, died during the early days of the pandemic."

I scowled. "Why didn't Cole step in then and spare his grandfather the extra work?"

Was the paragon my father had selected for me an inconsiderate germaphobe as well?

"You'll have to ask him that when you meet him, although that may not happen for quite a while. If Rayburn Enterprises successfully allied with Quaternity, it would be quite a coup for both companies."

Another win-win for Daddy.

"You mean like one of the old political and economic alliances between warring countries centuries ago?" I plopped onto my bed. With my nerves on edge as they were, I'd lost touch with my rational self. "Sacrificing some princess so that the king could reap the profits." I perked up. "Do I have a dowry? I'll bet it has to be a dang attractive one to get anyone to agree to wed and bed me. What am I worth? A billion or two? A treasure chest full of gold bullion and jewels? Some shares in the company? One of his other subsidiary companies? One of his top stud bulls? Ten years' worth of

Diablo's semen? Come on, you must know. Dan would've been the one to draw up the contract."

Amalia laughed. "You're hilarious. You missed your calling. Must you always look at the worst possible scenario? I would love to spend a day inside your head, seeing the world the way you do. I'm sure whichever man you choose will get something out of your marriage, but you won't come away with nothing, Daddy will see to that, and he'll see that your assets are protected. Rayburn Industries and Quaternity aren't warring. They aren't even in mild competition, but an alliance between them could open up a whole lot of new markets for our beef and our wine."

"Great. I always wanted to be someone's pathway to success. Every girl aspires to marry a man who's after her protected assets rather than her heart, but how will his absence tonight help?"

None of what she'd said had improved my mood.

Andressa sat, reached for my hand, and pulled me over to the bed once more.

"You aren't looking at this the right way, but enough of that for now. The fact that Cole won't be here can buy you more time, maybe as much as a year since if the elderly man doesn't recover, he'll be forced to assume the reins. If he hasn't been involved in the everyday business world, well, it's a steep learning curve."

I nodded. Given a year, I could work on Daddy, maybe take my shot at those few tweaks that would enhance my appearance. There was even a chance that I might find the man of my dreams if not my father's.

"That is assuming you don't like any of the men you meet tonight," she continued. "You can convince Daddy to let you travel a bit, either within the country or abroad, hang out with the people you enjoy spending time with, maybe even go to California and visit Ingrid and her husband." She winked. "I heard he does excellent work. When you're ready, if things don't work out the way you hope they will, you can come back to face him and Cole Rayburn."

It was as if Amalia had read my mind—either that or my diary. But I needed to be sure she was saying what I thought she was. I crossed my fingers. If she supported me…

"You mean go to LA and have a few tweaks done?"

I couldn't believe Amalia would condone that, especially when she knew how Daddy felt about plastic surgery. I couldn't imagine any of my half-sisters contradicting him and standing up to him for me.

She chuckled. "Sure, why not? If you feel that strongly about it, go for it. I went to Dallas and had a boob lift two months ago, and Alison and Aileen have both had collagen implants and tummy tucks in New York at the clinic their mother uses. With the amount of time she spends in the sun, Mom's had at least two facelifts. It's not a big deal. I'd bet my eyeteeth our newest stepmother's been to see a cosmetic surgeon, too. Daddy hasn't even noticed."

My jaw dropped. She couldn't be serious, but it did explain a few things.

Amalia laughed at the stunned look on my face. "Once you're married, you'll have more freedom than you realize. Daddy might notice your changes since they'll be a touch more dramatic, but once it's done, what can he do? Order you to undo them? Not likely, and if you agree to play nice and at least give Cole a chance…" She shrugged. "Come on, Cinderella. The photographer's waiting. Once he's taken his pictures, we really do have to get downstairs. Don't worry. We'll be there for you every step of the way."

Laughing, I nodded. "You never cease to surprise me. I wish I'd been born sooner. We could've had great times together."

She chuckled. "That's the nice thing about getting old. The years separating us tend to shrink. No reason why the four of us can't get into all kinds of fun together now." She reached for my hand. "I know how important your independence is to you, and the three of us will do whatever it takes to give you your chance to find happiness, but be careful. The world you see through those rose-colored glasses of yours can be an ugly place. If things don't work out, come home. And if all of these guys turn out to be duds, we'll do our best to convince Daddy to look elsewhere. But for now, we have your back, baby sister, and we always will."

I nodded, swallowing the lump in my throat and batting my eyelids once more to keep the tears away. I'd always loved and admired my half-sisters, and it awed me to realize they loved me, too.

* * *

By 11:30 p.m., I was dying, ready to gouge out my own eyes with a melon scoop if I thought it would get me out of here. I'd posed for enough pictures to be on the front page of every magazine and newspaper in the world. Daddy had introduced me to dozens of business associates whose names I would never remember. I'd thanked them for the generous donations they'd made to one of a half-dozen charities I'd selected as recipients of my birthday gifts—whatever I needed, I could buy myself. The absolute worst part of the evening was the unbearable amount of time I'd spent with each of the men my father had selected for me. If there was a Hell, it was here in this house tonight.

To their credit and my everlasting thanks, all of my half-sisters and brothers-in-law had taken turns rescuing me from one of Daddy's friends or one of the dismal suitors he'd picked for me. Even Aunt Raylene and Aunt Sophia had brought me temporary relief. Where were they now that I needed them more than ever? Daddy, Becki, and Cecily had all disappeared.

In all honesty, without someone's help, getting rid of this last guy would take an act of God like an earthquake or a tornado. If that didn't do it, then it was his death or mine. There wasn't a word in the English language to adequately describe the misery I felt. The more the jackanapes spoke, the more I wanted to open a can of whoopass on him or run from the room screaming, pulling my hair from my head, and rubbing the skin off my hands in an impersonation of Lady Macbeth driven to madness.

To make matters worse, he was allergic to horses, and the only animals he could tolerate were Chihuahuas—cute little dogs, it was true, but there was something about the image of a portly six-foot, sausage-fingered, two hundred and fifty pound man walking a Chihuahua in a raincoat and rainboots that just didn't work for me. Maybe he and Becki should compare notes on doggy clothing designers.

Desperate to get away if only for a few moments, I resorted to a lie.

"Leopold, I really need to use the powder room. I won't be long."

Before he could stop me, I slipped out the nearest door, but instead of going to the bathroom, I made my way to the sunroom, my asylum, the only room devoid of guests, dropped into a chair, and slipped off my shoes, sighing audibly at the temporary relief.

It wasn't silent in the dimly lit room, but it was far quieter, the party noises and music muffled by distance and closed doors, the open patio doors allowing the evening sounds to filter in. I could hear the soothing, rippling splash of the water in the corner fountain, a sound that never failed to calm me.

The door opened, and I shoved my shoes under the chair before shrinking back in it, terrified that the prince might've followed me here, a prince who considered himself a king now that his father had died ... a king without a country was apparently still a king, although people continued to refer to him as Prince Leopold.

I'd met a few of my father's royal acquaintances in the past when they'd come to the stables to buy a horse or some of a stallion's sperm, and while I'd found most of them to be self-centered and self-absorbed to a fault, looking down their noses at the people who catered to them, this one was the worst of the lot. If Daddy thought I'd marry this nincompoop just to be called Princess Andressa, he had another think coming.

In a generous mood, I might ascribe his bad manners to centuries of in-breeding and living in ancient, drafty castles full of black mold. To be honest, King Leopold, the heir to the non-existent throne of Dalcosta, a small country in south-central Europe, known for its wine and olives, was the most supercilious ass I'd ever met.

To begin with, he was delusional and spoke of himself in the first person plural, the royal we. He claimed what had happened to his father had been a misunderstanding formulated by his enemies. What was there to misunderstand? When Alison had dropped his name, I'd looked him up online. Where Cole Rayburn had no social presence, this fop had it in spades … more than five thousand pictures of himself, many of them showing him behaving badly.

Under family history, I'd discovered that his father had been a dictator who'd imprisoned everyone who'd disagreed with them. In his greed, he'd bled the country dry before eventually fleeing to Switzerland with his family—the army on his tail trying to get the country's treasury back. The prince would've been ten, just five years older than I was, but he didn't wear his age well.

According to what I'd read, a few months after his exile, the deposed king had fallen from a horse and broken his neck. As it turned out, that had been a lucky break since the Dalcostan government had ordered his arrest for grand larceny and treason. Luckily, the queen had quickly remarried a rich duke, who'd kept them all out of the poor house, and returned to Dalcosta. She'd sent Leopold to the UK for school, no doubt hoping that he'd marry into royalty there, but it hadn't panned out, and I could certainly understand why. Even the most desperate princess in the world deserved better.

Having failed in his attempt to secure a royal bride, Leopold was now trying his luck with what some considered American royalty, the less than 10 percent who controlled billions—not that I enjoyed being at the top of the list. Whatever Daddy saw in that man eluded me. When we sat down together in the morning, my father would have some explaining to do.

While the prince was well-dressed, his clothing tailored to him, he wasn't particularly attractive, especially with the signs of his life's dissipation all over him. He might only be thirty, but he looked at least ten years older. He was a heavy drinker—three glasses of champagne to my one—and he'd been at it all evening. The yellowish brown nicotine stains between his stubby, multi-ringed fingers, his foul breath, and the smoker's cough testified to vice number two. As well, he'd cornered me near the buffet table, eating on and off, mouth open while chewing, during our conversation that felt days rather than minutes long. My horses showed better table manners than that joker.

"Oh!" A shadow materializing beside me made me jump.

"I'm sorry. I didn't realize there was anyone in here."

The voice belonged to one of the waiters hired specifically for tonight. What was he doing in here? Casing the joint? The staff had all been vetted, but it was always possible they'd overlooked something.

"I was told this was the area we could use for our breaks. I'll leave."

Feeling like an idiot for jumping to conclusions, I shook my head.

"No, please. I'm the one who should apologize. Someone did say the staff had been given a place to rest. I should've realize since the room was empty that this was it. I'm the intruder. I'll go."

"Please, Ms. Myers, don't leave on my account. I've only got fifteen minutes, but I can go outside instead."

I couldn't place his accent, other than to say it definitely wasn't Texan or Southern, but his voice was a caress, the kind of soft, soothing voice that brought peace and tranquility, the very emotions lacking in the party's hustle and bustle.

"Please stay. I'm certain someone will have noticed my escape and come looking for me soon."

He laughed, the sound genuine and not forced.

"Don't tell me you aren't enjoying your own birthday party."

"Enjoying isn't the word I'd use, no. Tolerating, perhaps, but there's only so much of that," I waived my hand toward the door, "that I can take. It's just not me."

Using my feet, I rooted under the chair for my shoes, surprised when he bent down, scooped them out from under it, and handed them to me.

"Feet sore?"

"Yes," I mumbled. "I don't usually wear heels this high."

Before I could stop him, he pulled a chair closer to mine, lifted my feet into his lap, and started massaging the souls of my feet at the base of my toes.

I moaned. "Oh God, that feels so good. Where did you learn to do that?"

I was enjoying the foot massage far too much to make him stop.

"My grandmother was a teacher and spent hours on her feet. I learned what felt good. It seemed the least I could do since she'd done so much for me."

The man I'd secretly dubbed Handsome Harry had provided me with champagne once or twice and had kept Leopold well-lubricated. The white jacket, black shirt, white tie, and black pants with black shoes that allowed him to move silently around the room, didn't hide his broad shoulders and flat abdomen, a body characteristic often lacking in the party guests. He had blond hair that dusted the edge of his collar, a reddish blond mustache, and a neatly trimmed beard. In some ways, he resembled a young Robert Redford.

"If you aren't having a good time at your party, what would you rather be doing?"

"Seriously? Let's see—mucking out stalls comes to mind, but there's been enough manure tossed around here already."

He chuckled. "I've overheard more than my fair share of bull crap, but this is your party. If you didn't want all this, why do it?"

I'd give my eyeteeth to have him as one of the four, to be able to dance and converse with him rather than with my father's sycophants. He was easy to talk to, a quality rarely found in the social circles I was forced to frequent, and if the way he massaged my feet were any indication, he could probably make my body sing.

"Believe me, if I'd been asked, I would've refused, but then you wouldn't have a job tonight, and one of us should get something out of this. In truth, it's my father's cattle auction, and I'm the one in the ring with the buyers circling."

I reached for my shoes, but he gently grasped my feet again—my own Prince Charming sliding the slipper on his Cinderella. I stood, slightly embarrassed but definitely grateful. If he wanted to give up waitering, he could probably make a good living massaging feet.

"Thank you. That's much better. I'm sorry about ruining your break this way. Whiny, needy girl isn't usually my M O. I'm tougher than that. Let's just say I'd rather be delivering twin calves than be here tonight."

"You're a vet?" He seemed surprised.

"Educated and certified, but I only practice on the ranch. I look after Quaternity's stock. Not a very ladylike occupation, but I begged Daddy to let me study veterinary medicine, and since he was busy with his new wife of the moment, he was happy to indulge me and keep me away. I attended Cornell."

"Impressive. Still, it doesn't seem like the actions of a loving father to me. Let you have your dream but limit your use of it."

It was my turn to laugh. "Daddy's definition of love and mine are a little cattywampus. I was okay with it until tonight, but my problems aren't yours."

I walked over to the open doors, the sound of the fountain louder now. How many times had I stood here with Mama, inhaling the scent of the garden? I missed her more than ever.

Handsome Harry followed me, the pleasant aroma of his spicy aftershave blending with the scent of the roses in the garden below us.

"It's like an oasis in the desert," he mused.

"My mother had the gardens designed when she moved into this house. There's plenty of water in the ground here, water that flooded some of the older oil wells, so she had irrigation pipes put in to keep the flowers and grass alive. There were two things about this place she loved, her horses and her flowers. Growing up in Brazil and living there until she married Daddy made this landscape quite a surprise."

"You surprise me. You aren't at all what I expected."

I smiled. "Neither are you."

CHAPTER THREE

"And what did you expect me to be?" His words were clipped.

Had I insulted him? I hadn't meant to.

I put my hand on his sleeve, the heat of his body flowing through it, sending pleasant ripples up my arm. Dang it. I liked this guy. Too bad nothing could come of it.

"Whatever you think I meant, that's not it. What I meant was so kind and helpful. You wasted your break rubbing my feet. That's the nicest thing anyone has done for me in a long time, but let me guess. You expected a rich, spoiled, socialite all wrapped up in herself and her money. That isn't my style, at least it's not the one I want, nor is that the kind of person I try to be, but after tonight, it's out of my hands. He'll make his choice, and that'll be that."

"Why don't you say no and leave?"

I laughed. "Do you really think it's that easy for someone like me to just run away? My face is all over the press. I might want my freedom, but there are those out there who would see me as a pay check, and I wouldn't be the only one to suffer. I can't walk away from who I am, but if I could, I would in a shot. I may not like it, but this is my lot in life."

There was no need to say anything more, and he seemed to understand that.

Besides, I sucked at small talk. Unlike Amalia and the twins whose mothers had sent then to finishing school to polish their perfect manners and conversational skills, Mama had ingrained in me the need to trust myself, my abilities, and be self-sufficient. When I'd turned up my nose at ballet, much to Daddy's dismay, she'd taught me to ride, rope, and break broncos the way she had in Brazil, working on her father's horse ranch, claiming it hadn't stopped him from marrying her. Of course, she'd realized that the 50 percent share of that ranch, enough to start his own breeding stable, might've had something to do with it.

As a child, I'd had two favorite books, Hans Christian Andersen's *The Ugly Duckling* and *The Paper Bag Princess* by Robert Munsch. By the time I was twelve, I'd given up all expectations of ever becoming a swan, but the other story held out hope for me. In *The Paper Bag Princess*, Princess Elizabeth had lost everything—her home, her fancy clothes, and the prince she loved to a mean dragon. With her fine gown gone, she'd clothed herself in a paper bag and had gone off to rescue Ronald, the captured prince. With her quick intellect, she outsmarted the dragon, but when Ronald saw her, instead of being happy and grateful that she'd risked it all to rescue him, he insulted her clothes and her abilities and told her to go away and come back when she looked like a real princess. At that moment, she realized the importance of standing up for herself, and not letting the opinions and attitudes of others define her. She skipped off into the sunset alone, and I knew that she was going to be just fine.

I'd wanted to be like Elizabeth and had done a fair job of it … riding as well as any of the wranglers and learning to swim thanks to Aunt Sophia who'd been an Olympic gold medal winner years ago. I'd thrown myself into junior rodeoing, capturing ribbons and trophies, but then Mama died, shattering that dream, Daddy sent me away to Our Lady of Perpetual Sorrows, an exclusive Catholic boarding school near Buffalo, New York. Instead of a paper bag and a sword, I wore burgundy and white uniforms and stuffed my face with pasta and bread. The dreaded dragon had won the battle, and I lost the me I loved in a crowd of strangers, gaining weight and retreating inside myself.

Eventually, the pain eased, the dietician controlled my meals, the physical education teacher put me through my paces in the gym, I started riding again on the school's property, and grew my own thick dragon-scaled skin. By the end of my senior year, my body was a far cry from my taller, slender peers, but I was reasonably fit and close to Ingrid whose father had gotten rich on the life insurance and court settlement he'd gotten when his wife had been killed in an industrial accident. Wanting a better life for himself, he'd sent his daughter into exile, just like me.

"There you are," Becki said, her tone filled with disdain. "Leopold is looking all over for you, and here you are cavorting with the help." She shook her head and turned to my companion. "You're being paid to serve drinks, not flirt with my step-daughter."

Handsome Harry smiled. "Yes, ma'am. I've just finished my break. Ms. Myers, enjoy the rest of your party."

"Thank you," I mumbled, mortified, wishing the floor would open and swallow me whole.

I watched the man walk away.

"You were rude," I stated, fisting my hands at my side and turning my back to her to stare outside once more, whatever calmness I'd achieved gone.

She grabbed my arm. "Don't turn your back on me! I'm not the one who was rude. You walked away from a prince, a real prince, who could well be a king one day. He said you went to the powder room, and I find you in here doing God knows what with a waiter. Seriously. I was told you were the smart, amenable one. Have you no idea how important tonight is?"

I thought of what Amalia had said about Mama's comment on my temper. One of these days, I would pop my cork, and I was afraid that day might be soon, but tonight, as usual, I swallowed my ire.

"Believe me, Becki, no one knows what's at stake here tonight more than I do. I needed air and a few minutes to myself." I pulled away from her and Cecily. Did that dang dog even know how to walk? She carried the thing all over the place. "You of all people should know I'm not a party girl. You may be my father's sixth wife, but you have nothing to say in the way I conduct myself. I'm twenty-five years old. You're twenty-seven. For Daddy's sake and that of harmony, I've done my best to be nice to you and your dog, but I really don't need maternal advice from you, nor do I need your mind in the gutter. We were just talking. Since when is it a sin to talk to someone? Now, I'd best get back."

Straightening my spine, pretending it and my feet weren't killing me, and that I was looking forward to the next two hours, I turned my back on her once more and returned to the party, stopping off at the powder room on my way.

"There you are, darling," Leopold cried, drawing the attention of those around us. "We've missed you."

I smiled and shrugged, digging deep inside me for my acting ability.

The band played a slow song, one I recognized as Mama's favorite.

Leopold set down his plate and his glass and turned to me.

"Shall we dance, Andressa?"

Knowing I had no choice in the matter, I set down my glass and let him lead me onto the dance floor.

How much more torture would I have to endure before this night was over? I caught a glimpse of Handsome Harry circulating with a tray of champagne. If only…

Moving around the dance floor with Prince Leopold was the worst form of torture. With the exception of one other, the men I'd danced with this evening had known what they were doing. Not so this buffoon. Had he skipped out on the obligatory dance lessons that would've been part of his training as a boy in order to visit an all-you-can-eat buffet or the royal kitchens to sip the cooking sherry? Were his balance and dance skills further casualties of the champagne he'd consumed?

He held me closer than I liked, his musky body odor warring with a cheap, flowery cologne, making me long for Handsome Harry's pleasant, spicy scent. Fancying himself a crooner, Leopold insisted on singing off-key, his words to the song not quite the lyrics made famous in the sixties by The Animals. He stumbled every now and then, jostling dancers, and smashing my toes to the sounds of the orchestra's instrumental version of "The House of the Rising Sun."

Given he was 0 for 3, what other foibles did he espouse? He might be a prince, but if he'd been the frog one, while I disliked frogs' legs, I would've taken him home and turned him into dinner—frog ratatouille, frog fricassee, or some similar concoction—doing my good deed for the citizens of Dalcosta and single women everywhere.

When the music mercifully ended, I limped off the floor. Handsome Harry stood there with a trayful of champagne, and I reached for a glass. It wasn't anesthetic, but a few more glasses might numb the pain. Leopold grabbed two, although I doubted he was in pain, guzzled one, and set the empty glass back on the tray. Given the glazed look in his eyes, if I were lucky, he just might pass out somewhere and spare me the dishonor of his company … or another dance since I was concerned I might have a few broken toes.

Spying an empty chair, I moved toward it, but Leopold reached for my hand, preventing me from escaping. Giving one last longing glance at the empty seat, I sighed and turned back to him, praying for the patience and fortitude to tolerate him a few minutes longer. Mama would expect me to behave like a lady.

"Ms. Myers?"

I looked over my shoulder and saw Handsome Harry, his chocolate brown eyes filled with compassion. He placed the chair I desperately wanted next to me. The man had anticipated my needs just by glancing at me. How absolutely perfect was that?

"Thank you, so much." I melted into the chair, ignoring the way Leopold glared at the man.

He looked at him as if he were some sort of germ on a microscope slide. "We'll have a chair, too," he ordered.

Handsome Harry smiled. "I'm sorry, sir, but that's the only available one." With that, he slid back into the crowd.

Leopold harrumphed. "Cheeky bastard." He looked down at me, examined the chair, and then lifted his gaze to mine. "Are you sure you need to sit?"

Was he seriously expecting me to get up and give him my chair?

Not on your life, buddy.

"Just for a little while. I'm not used to these shoes."

"Then, why not just take them off? We're sure the floor would be suitably comforting under your feet. In fact, we could sit on the chair, and while you're a bit chubbier than we like our women, you aren't too heavy. You could sit on our lap for a few moments. We could discuss the first thing that came up."

My eyes opened wide. He'd just insulted me and made a crude joke in the same sentence. The man wasn't just a drunk, he was a bad-mannered oaf.

Had I been a cartoon character, I'm certain my face would've turned puce, and smoke would've shot out of my ears. Steeling myself, trying to recall Mama's admonition to say nothing if I couldn't say something nice, I shook my head.

"I'm afraid that's not possible. My mama always said a lady keeps her shoes on at a party, so I can't possibly take them off. While this may be my birthday party, unless you're Santa Claus, my sitting on your lap would be frowned upon."

He laughed, reached for another smoked oyster, popped it into his mouth, and grinned.

"You are a delightful blend of the modern, working woman and the prim, proper obedient one. That's exactly why we and our country need you." He swallowed and reached for a caviar-topped cracker. "Andressa, we're certain that our union will be of great benefit to us and to you. We have no doubt that with your father's generous backing and his promise to establish a variety of new industries in our realm, we can reclaim our throne. With you as our queen, our people will clamor for our return."

Our union? Talk about putting the cart before the horse. We'd met an hour ago—minus the fifteen minutes I'd spent with Handsome Harry—and while it felt like an eternity, it wasn't. Was he really so out of touch with reality that he believed I would accept him as a husband? I narrowed my eyes. Could it be possible that Alison was wrong, and this fool had somehow convinced Daddy to back him and not Cole?

I wanted to barf. The thought of being this man's queen was enough to make me side with the peasants and start a second revolution. I could see myself carrying a pitchfork and running through the cobblestoned streets screaming, "Off with his head."

"I honestly don't think I'd make a very good queen," I stated, hoping to let him down easy. "As an American, I've already waged war against one king and won."

He guffawed as if I'd made some fantastic joke, drawing the attention of those around us once more.

"Darling, you have the most wonderful sense of humor. Don't you see the irony of it? With you by our side, pledging your undying love and devotion, the people will recognize our superiority and beg us to rule them. It's not as if they're better off with the measly rights they've accorded themselves. We will be merciful, only dealing harshly with those who deposed our father. After all, the masses are weak-minded and easily swayed. They'll believe whatever we tell them and beg for more."

I almost swallowed my tongue in an effort to keep from saying something tremendously undiplomatic. I couldn't for the life of me see how King Leopold had made his way into the Matrimonial Stakes. It was as if Daddy had scraped the bottom of the barrel, checked the refuse, and then looked deeper, pulling out the lowest of the low.

He wanted a grandson, something none of his other daughters had given him, but if he thought this man and I could do so, he'd lost his mind. I wouldn't let this poor excuse for a human being touch me, let alone screw me.

As I pretended to listen to him drone on about the changes he had planned for his restored kingdom, it occurred to me that not one of the four men I'd met had any of the qualities I might consider essential or at least desirable in a husband. The waiter was far more to my liking than his choices, although to be fair, Cole Rayburn had ingratiated himself by his absence. It seemed that Daddy didn't know me at all.

The first one, Lincoln Ford, a tall, thin, balding man in his mid-thirties, the great-grandnephew of a past president, a man who'd made his millions in the auto industry, had been impeccably dressed but carried a distinct aroma about him, one that was familiar to me since I spent hours in the stables almost every day. The man fancied himself an inventor, claiming to have hundreds of patents pending, anyone of which could make him richer than he already was. Did I mention he was modest?

Not! He flouted his so-called genius and his family's roots and money. In some ways, he reminded me of Sheldon from *The Big Bang Theory*, completely oblivious to social conventions but without a single redeeming quality.

I was ready to run out of the room screaming after listening to him for a full half-hour described the strange inventions he was working on, everything from self-cleaning, recyclable diapers, toilets that turned urine into potable water, and feces-powered engines. The man was obsessed with waste. He believed the world was overlooking a valuable commodity and source of energy by ignoring refuse from humans.

"Think of it, Andressa. People and animals eat and defecate. Over the century, animal feces have been used as fertilizer, fuel, even a base for such things as adobe bricks, and yet, what have we done with human feces? We've done our best to get rid of them. But what if we combined it with the animal excrement? We would have a perpetual source of renewable energy. We could replace coal-powered

plants, possibly even nuclear plants without the danger of radioactive fallout."

He was quite excited about gaining access to our manure piles, anticipating the tons of fecal matter my stable and the cattle barns could provide annually. I'd wager that he was more interested in cow dung than marrying me.

When Aileen had rescued me from him by bringing over Nataly Raynes, a woman I knew would be interested in Lincoln's fat wallet, I was so grateful to her that I could've kissed her. Nataly was welcome to him, and her father's stores of cow patties were just as great as mine.

Unfortunately, my relief had been short-lived. Daddy had escorted bachelor number two to my side. Lyle Portsmouth, the son of one of the oilmen he knew well and had worked with for years, hadn't been into poop, human or otherwise. The renowned playboy with the biggest online presence of them all, rambled on about the places he'd been, the people he'd met, and the extreme sports he adored. He'd begged me to introduce him to Aunt Sophia and her husband, claiming to have participated in several of their exotic adventures, probably hoping the familiarity would get him exclusivity.

He'd taken great pains describing how he'd stalked a lion, armed only with a camera and a tranquilizer gun with one dart. Too bad the lion hadn't been armed, too. He'd climbed K2, the second peak in the Karakoram Range, spending some time describing how he'd learned to crush grubs and worms into a tasty and acceptable meat substitute, and he'd been kayaking on the Amazon River. Who knew that piranha were edible?

"A little salty, fishy, maybe a trifle ripe but delicious with mango chutney."

Knowing of my interest in horses, he'd suggested we go to Camargue, France, search for the famed, wild, white horses, many of the animals still living and protected in the Camargue National Park, which included a UNESCO designated biosphere reserve, and try to rope and ride them. Even if it were legal, that would be the last thing I would ever do to such majestic animals.

After I'd professed no interest in participating in that or any similar activities, he'd barely said ten words to me, spending the rest of our allotted time together letting his gaze roam the crowd and settle on one pretty girl after the other. Even when we danced, he held me as if I had leprosy, not that I minded, but his eyes were fixed on the butts or bosoms of each woman who came near us.

Desperate to be rid of him, I'd signaled Aunt Sophia and made the introduction. As always, she'd been her gracious self. She'd saved me by offering to introduce him to Lettie Carver, a cattle baron's daughter who also used their services. Praise God! To me, a man constantly putting his life in danger, especially one with a roving eye, definitely wasn't husband material.

Candidate number three, Jackson Hickman, a cattle rancher from Montana who hoped to win one of the two congressional seats up for grabs this year, wasn't my type. Far from it. If a man could embody all the character traits I despised, he was it. He saw himself as God's gift to women and this nation, a man who would help reshape this country, no doubt at the expense of the little guy. Aware of my interest in horses, he bragged about bagging a couple of mustangs in the Pryor Mountains. His words as well as his attitude were branded in my memory.

"I thought it was illegal to own a feral horse in Montana," I stated primly, knowing that the entire herd amounted to little more than a hundred and sixty horses.

"I've got a friend on the BLM, the Bureau of Land Management. He let me know it was time to cull the herds, and I helped out. They aren't broken yet. Might be something you'd like to do." He smiled. "Shot myself a bison while I was at it, too. Just a cow, but a kill is a kill."

"That's legal?"

"Damn right it is. They cross out of Yellowstone Park. Montana doesn't welcome brucellosis-carrying animals in our state. One sick bison can infect cattle, horses, and sheep, even

spreading to dogs and humans. It was a community service."

"Yes," I agreed, as a vet, well aware of the dangers of brucellosis. It could decimate a herd. Did the cow have it?"

"Nah, she was clean and made good eating. If you come up to Montana after the election, I should have time to take you out hunting. We've got deer, elk, bear, and of course, the odd bison."

He'd laughed and then had bragged about the fact that he'd killed something in every state. Jackson had gone on and on about how much he'd enjoyed his whale hunting venture in Japan and how much he looked forward to another such trip, this time to Iceland. He'd pointed to his alligator boots and belt, claiming he'd slain the animal for them himself, and then had spent far too much time on his hunting prowess of everything from dispatching Polar bears in Alaska to spearing reef sharks in Zanzibar. It wasn't that I was anti-hunting since I enjoyed venison, but killing for the sake of killing, for the *fun of it*, had never appealed.

To make matters even worse, Jackson was a dirty old man—well not that old, maybe forty-five—but he was definitely a pig, a boar of the first order. He'd been all over me like flies on a cow patty. He'd made several inappropriate and off-color comments about some of the women at the party, not all of them unmerited, but when we'd danced, he'd crushed me so tightly to him that I was certain the imprint of his fancy belt buckle would leave a mark on my belly.

I'd had to use all the strength I could muster to push away from him so that I could breathe. As if that wasn't bad enough, I had to pull his hand off my ass before he decided to check me for hemorrhoids.

He'd guaranteed that I would fight tooth and nail not to marry him with his final comment when we'd left the dance floor.

"The electorate like their candidates married, maybe with a kid or a bun in the oven. I like you. Your father says you're a vet, which would save me money. Make you useful as well as decorative. You

don't talk too much, and you've got meat on your bones. The best women have wide hips for childbearing and a little cushioning, so a man doesn't get bruised pelvic bones grinding into them. Looking forward to planting my seeds in you and growing a crop of little Hickmans of my own."

His boisterous laughter had brought Amalia and Dan to my side, with Jessica Limpet, recently divorced from husband number three. Oversexed, with all the curves he could possibly want and the morals of an alley cat, her come-hither look and his leer sealed my release. Unfortunately, that had opened the door for Leopold.

I turned back to suitor number four, now gorging himself on a warm canape from a woman's tray. I was all out of small talk and dreaded listening to more of his.

The aroma of Becki's perfume approached before she did.

"Andressa, darling, your father is ready to have you cut the cake." She eyed Leopold as if he was a steak, and she hadn't eaten in months.

I grinned, giving her what was probably the first genuine smile I'd ever given her, forgiving her earlier behavior tonight. If God had sent her to my rescue, then I could be magnanimous.

"Right away."

She gave Leopold the once over and then turned to go back the way she'd come, her ass swaying back and forth, her poodle dressed in a matching pink sequined dress that had probably cost more than the gown I wore.

Standing, I turned to the prince and stifled my smile. "I'm sorry, but I have to go. Feel free to sit. It—"

He cut me off before I could dismiss him permanently.

"It's not a problem. We'll come with you. We're quite fond of cake."

I smiled weakly. "Of course you are."

Using every ounce of self-control I could muster, I crossed the room, the prince walking so closely behind me that he could well have been my shadow. I could smell the oysters he'd consumed on his fetid breath. As soon as I saw Daddy, I exhaled and moved more quickly. Alison stepped between me and the prince, effectively blocking his approach.

Sitting on the table was a huge slab cake, marble with white icing, *Happy Birthday Andressa* written on it in bright pink letters, surrounded by twenty-five lit candles set in candy roses. Beside it sat a fancy Japanese fan and a basket for cards. Members of the catering staff stood nearby with a variety of ice cream to add to the cake.

The band played, and the crowd joined in the singing of the obligatory "Happy Birthday" song, the one I'd always felt sounded more like a funeral dirge than a celebratory song, but actually seemed appropriate now.

Picking up the fan, I opened it and proceeded to waive it back and forth to put out the candles. One of the things learned during the pandemic was that blowing out birthday candles was a great way to spread germs.

I reached for the knife Daddy handed me and cut the cake down the center to the applause of friends and family.

Swallowing my nerves, I moved away from the table and over to the podium beside my father, well away from Daddy's crop of potential husbands. I needn't have worried. The first three were involved in conversation with other women, and Becki and Cecily were keeping the prince company, proof in my book that Jesus loved me, and Mama was looking out for me.

Heart pounding, I stepped up to the mic.

"Good evening. I want to thank you all so much for coming, and especially for making your generous donations. It warms my heart to know that so many causes will benefit from this day." I might be miserable, but if those in need got something from this, then it was worth the sacrifice. I swallowed and continued. "The cake is self-serve, so come forward, pick your flavor of ice cream, and enjoy what I know will be a delicious treat. The band has one more set, there's lots of food and champagne left, so please have fun." After all, it was a party. "Before you leave, don't forget to grab one of the gift boxes by the exit. And once again, thank you all for helping me celebrate this momentous day."

People applauded once more and started to move toward the table.

I stepped away and turned to my father. Somehow, he looked older, frailer, maybe even a little sadder tonight. Was he thinking of Mama, too?

"Thank you, Daddy. It was a lovely party."

He frowned and leaned toward me, lowering his voice.

"I'd hoped you would meet someone special tonight, but it appears that they're otherwise occupied. Damn shame when a man walks away from a thoroughbred and settles for a nag."

Okay. I'd moved up from being a prized cow to being a prized horse. It was an improvement, right?

I swallowed and pasted a smile on my face. "They are. What more could I want than to see people happy and enjoying themselves tonight, helping me celebrate this special birthday?" The last thing I wanted to do was argue about this now. "Can we talk about this later? I need to use the powder room."

Lips pursed, he nodded.

"I'll come with." Amalia reached for my arm. "We can get our cake after the others have theirs."

He was about to say something else when Aunt Raylene stepped in.

"Wallis, it was so nice of you to arrange for all of this. Anya would've been so proud of…"

She pulled him toward the table, her words lost in the noise from the crowd.

"Come on," Amalia stated, dragging me away. "Aunt Raylene will keep him busy for a while. We don't want the fat prince to corner you again."

CHAPTER FOUR

I hurried after Amalia, terrified that my tired ankles would fold in on themselves, and that I would collapse halfway to the bathroom. Instead of going to the main floor powder room, we climbed the stairs and went into my room.

She closed the door behind us and exhaled. Pointing to the bathroom door, she smiled and dropped onto the side of the bed as she had earlier, but this time she removed her shoes and rubbed her feet against the plush carpet.

"Go first."

I followed suit before disappearing into the en suite bathroom, grateful that I could actually walk.

It seemed the damage the prince had inflicted on my toes was minor, and the benefit my soles had gotten from Handsome Harry's ministrations was still in play.

A few minutes later when I returned, Alison and Aileen had joined Amalia. Alison wore a powder blue peau de soie gown that cinched her small waist, while Aileen's dress was a silk, emerald-green, backless sheath with a thigh-high slit. In front of them sat a wheeled tray covered with a large silver dome.

"Did I miss a note or something?" I joked, trying to cover up my confusion. I couldn't recall a time when all three of my sisters had been in my room with me.

Alison, the eldest, born an hour and twenty minutes before Aileen, shook her head, and walked over to me, her grin almost splitting her face.

"No, cupcake."

She used the nickname she'd given me all those years ago, one that might've been more suitable for a young child than an adult, but as silly as it sounded, it made me feel special and brought back pleasant memories of having Mama around. My nieces had given me another, Aunt Dressa, since Aunt Andressa had been too big a mouthful for them.

"We wanted to surprise you. It occurred to me the other day that, as sisters, we'd never had the opportunity to do much together. We've never even had cake and ice cream just the four of us. Amalia and I arranged for the staff to bring up four pieces when Aileen signaled. Amalia wasn't sure how she would get you up here, but you provided the perfect excuse. Mom promised to keep Daddy distracted, but we have to get you back downstairs for the last dance. By the way, Anderson's brother, Garret, will step in to dance with you before any of the other men do."

My eyes grew large. Was she tossing her brother-in-law into the ring?

She laughed. "Don't look at me like that. He's a fifty-five-year-old priest. He's not a threat. Here's your surprise. I hope you'll like it."

She lifted the silver dome to reveal four slices of cake, each one topped with the chocolate confection that was my absolute favorite.

"How? Where? When?" I seemed unable to utter anything but one-syllable words.

"It wasn't easy getting *brigadeiro*. Anderson had it flown in earlier today from Rio. I remembered how much you and Aunt Anya loved it."

Blinking wasn't enough to stop the tears.

"Don't cry," Aileen ordered. The twins weren't identical, but they bore a striking resemblance to each other. "We wanted you to enjoy at least one thing tonight."

Had they all known how miserable the thought of this party had made me?

"I'm not sad. It's just … this is the nicest thing..."

Alison put her arm around my shoulders. "Hey, we may not always have shown it, Andressa, but you're our baby sister, and we love you. We want you to be happy. Remember that. Whatever we do, we do out of love. Try it."

I reached for my plate and dug my fork into the frozen fudge-like ball of condensed milk, chocolate, and butter. A groan of pure pleasure escaped me.

"Oh, God. It's been so long since I've had this, and it's perfect, just like Mama used to make."

"There's more in the kitchen freezer," Aileen added. "We didn't mention it to the kids, or it would've been gone by now."

"Maybe I should share it. At three-hundred and fifty calories per serving..." I chuckled. "Two of my delightful suitors commented on my weight as it is. I'd better watch myself."

Amalia burst out laughing. "Do tell! Which clowns were so rude?"

I repeated some of Jackson's statement, the least offensive parts of it, and followed it with the prince's before turning my attention back to the dessert.

"Well, of all the low-down, bad-mannered varmints." Aileen shook her head. "As if their opinion should matter! I wasn't impressed with either man before this, and I'm even less so now." She forked some of the dessert from her plate into her mouth and swallowed. "Mmm, this is heavenly. Why is it that men can let themselves go, but it a woman just teeters on the brink of imperfection … I am so sick of this idiotic double standard."

"It's okay, Aileen." As always, I was willing to swallow an insult to keep the peace. I didn't want anything to ruin this moment. "I've long since accepted that I'm not up to standard, but this… This has made my day. It's as if Mama is here celebrating with me, too."

I took another forkful of cake and *brigadeiro*, savoring the sweetness.

"You are too kind to others and far too hard on yourself. I hope that … that things work out for you." I sensed Aileen wanted to say more, but she took another bite of her dessert instead.

For a few moments, silence filled the room as we indulged ourselves.

Alison finished her plate first and set it down on the tray.

"We don't have much longer before we have to get back, but we need to talk. Having spent far less time with each of the men Daddy chose for you than you did, we're worried. Those men may be rich—although I think that prince is nothing but a contemptible, insufferable, carpetbagger—but none of them is suitable husband material, and we all know it. Jackson Hickman's addiction to killing anything that moves gave me the willies, and as far as Lyle Portsmouth's concerned, that man is all hat, no cattle. I wouldn't believe he'd done all those things he bragged about if you showed me the pictures. He's far too lily-livered to put his life at risk. Did you look at his hands? As Mom would say, those hands haven't done a lick's worth of work. His manicure is as fine as they come. Lincoln Ford may come from good stock and be richer than Midas, but there is something wrong with him. Was it just me, or did he smell like manure?"

Aileen laughed. "It wasn't just you. Richard said he found him checking out the midden behind the stable. Probably tracked that dung all through the house."

I giggled. That explained it.

Alison picked up the thread of conversation again.

"Daddy's mild stroke last year scared the bejesus out of all of us. He looks fine, but he's different. It's changed him and not for the better. He's impulsive, short-tempered, and downright crotchety. Laura's only twenty, and he's already making noises about finding her a suitable husband. If the ones he chose for you are his idea of suitable, well … Let's face it, he's wrong, and that's not the worst of it. Marrying Becki was out of character for him, and while amalgamating her father's steel companies with ours was a shrewd business move, Anderson assures me that it could've been done without the nuptials."

"Dan agrees with that," Amalia added. "The pre-nup is very similar to the others, so she'll get well-paid for servicing him, but nothing more. Two years is the longest he's ever been unwed, so I suppose it was just a matter of time. Don't get me wrong. Maybe he was just lonely, and she is quite pretty even though there are times when I think that dog of hers has more sense than she does. I definitely like her better than Charlotte or Desiree, but that isn't saying much."

Aileen shook her head. "We're off topic here, but the point is, he's not making sound business decisions. Anderson and Dan think it's time for him to retire, and Richard agrees."

This was beginning to sound like a mutiny. The captain of the ship's abilities were questionable, and it was time for him to go.

I frowned. Did he sense it? Did he feel the way Leopold's father felt when his ministers and generals deposed him? Was that why he empathized with the son? I shook my head. No, this wasn't like that. It couldn't be.

Alison saw the gesture and frowned.

"I know it's hard to hear, but be honest, Andressa. You spend more time with him than any of us. You must've seen this all-consuming need he has for a grandson. Good grief. It isn't as if that child will even carry the Myers name. Seeing the men he invited here tonight, the men he thinks best suited for you makes us shudder. As far as we're concerned, not one of the Freaky Four is proper husband material. Are we right?"

I nodded. At least I wasn't the only one who thought so. Handsome Harry flitted through my thoughts. He would do nicely, but Daddy would never accept him. I wasn't even sure the girls would. They wanted me happy, yes, but with a member of the class they approved.

"You can't choose one of them, and given the odds, bachelor number five won't be a heck of a lot better, although I can't imagine he could be worse."

Amalia burst out laughing. When we all looked at her, she swallowed her giggles.

"I was just trying to picture worse," she explained. "Maybe all four rolled into one?"

Aileen shook her head. "So, what are we going to do about it? You can't let him saddle you with any of those men."

I chuckled. "Funny, and here I thought it was the other way around."

She harrumphed. "Don't be silly. You're a smart, attractive woman who will be the perfect companion for the right man, not one of those here tonight. I know you're all hung up over your appearance, but it only took a little makeup to have you looking fantastic. So, to repeat my question. What are you, or rather we, going to do about it?"

I stared at my sisters and chewed my lower lip. How was I going to answer that question? I knew what I wanted to do, even had a vague plan for achieving the anonymity I needed, but wanting to do something and actually doing it were lightyears apart.

I needed to get away from here and find myself, find what made me happy, and while I loved being a vet and dealing with the horses, I was convinced there was something else out there for me, something wonderful and exciting, if I could only grab the brass ring.

I didn't want any of Daddy's choices, the elusive Cole Rayburn included. I wanted someone down to earth and caring, someone like Handsome Harry, a man who'd massaged my sore feet and had made me feel good about myself, if only for a little while. But it couldn't be him because he knew I was Andressa Myers, billionaire heiress. I wanted to be someone else. I needed to be someone else for my plan to find true love to work.

But leaving the sanctuary of Quaternity Ranch was no easy feat, and it could be risky. In the past, girls of my ilk had been kidnapped and held for ransom. At university, in my first year psych classes, I'd written a paper on Patty Hearst and Stockholm Syndrome. The heiress had been kidnapped fifty years ago, turned by her SLA captors, had denounced her wealthy status, and robbed banks with them. She was arrested, sentenced to seven years in prison, ended up marrying the police officer who'd guarded her while her case was in appeal, and eventually had been pardoned by President Clinton. It was a fear we all lived with, one that had Daddy insisting we never go anywhere alone.

It hadn't been much of an issue at boarding school, the grounds secure at all times, not because of me but because of others, like the daughter of an emir, a few minor British royals, and a senator's daughter attending the school. I'd lived in a secure apartment while I'd been a student at Cornell and had been driven to and from school every day. One of my classmates was a private detective charged with my safety. She graduated the same day I did and now worked in a pet hospital in Ithaca, having married the vet she'd worked with. If she could find a guy and fall in love, why couldn't I?

Before I could answer, Amalia stood beside me.

"Knowing Andie, she's been giving this a lot of thought and probably has a plan. We're going to help her with it." She reached for my hand and cupped hers over it. "The Four Musketeers swore an oath of loyalty to stand by one another at all times. Let's do the same. Remember the words?"

Aileen and Alison covered her hand.

"Yup," they answered as one.

Amalia smiled. "Here goes. Say it with me."

Together, we intoned, "All for one, and one for all."

Handsome Harry had asked me why I wouldn't say no and leave. Because I'd been afraid, but now, maybe I could take that first step—with their help and a whole lot of luck.

"So what's your plan?" Aileen crossed her arms.

I swallowed. "I want some plastic surgery, not a lot, just enough to fix things so that I don't have to plaster on the warpaint each day and eye surgery so that I can ditch the glasses and contact lenses. Then, I want a new identity and a job, not a vet since I would need to get registered and without credentials in my new name, it wouldn't work, but something where I'd meet a lot of people. Then, with all that in place, I could find my own husband, a man who'll love me for who I am, not what I am and the size of my bank account."

Amalia let out a deep breath. "That's a pretty tall order, but it's more or less what I expected," she admitted, glancing at the twins. "And I have an idea how we can pull it off, but you'll have to follow my lead. If it works out the way I hope it will, we can buy you a year—four months for the surgery to heal and eight months to find your perfect mate. It isn't a lot, but I doubt we can convince Daddy to give you more. I'll fill you all in later, but right now, we have to get back downstairs for the last dance." She grinned. "Cheer up, Andie. You're about to get your cake and a fork to eat it."

Slipping my feet back into my shoes, I followed my sisters down the stairs, more excited than I'd been all night. I looked around for Handsome Harry, but the waiter was nowhere to be seen, no doubt in the kitchen helping pack up all the plates, pans, and glassware the catering firm had brought with them. Too bad. I would've loved to have been able to give him my news—not that it would've been a smart move since no one could know what I was doing.

Entering the main party room, I saw Daddy searching the crowd, a relieved look on his face when he spotted me. Had he thought I wouldn't make it back?

"Here she is." My father held out his hand to me. "I'd thought I'd have this dance with you since I had the first, but someone suggested I should dance with my wife. So, Father Garret Steele will escort you around the floor. Becki? Where are you, sugar?"

Becki hurried over, looking slightly disheveled, but then she liked her champagne, and it had been a long night.

My father shook his head, his brow creased.

"For heaven's sake, put the dog down while we dance."

I expected her to argue with my father's order, but she handed Cecily to Lawrence, our butler. I knew for a fact that he disliked dogs, but he didn't flinch or move a muscle.

The band surprised me by having a singer join them. They played "Fortnight" by Taylor Swift, my favorite recording artist as well as a woman I admired.

Father Garret was an excellent dancer, and as soon as the music ended, he led me to the door to bid all the guests adieu and saved me from having to spend any more time with the Freaky Four as Alison had called them.

Once the guests had all left to be chauffeured home or to nearby hotels, Amalia whispered in my ear.

"Go to bed. You're plum tuckered out, as we all are. Dan and I are staying over, since he and Daddy have a meeting tomorrow in Midland. Antonia went home with Rose, Alison's daughter. They get along really well. It's too late to talk strategy now. The other musketeers and I will see you in your office in the stables after lunch. Love you, Andie."

With that she hurried over to Dan, and they climbed the stairs hand in hand.

I hesitated. Could I find Handsome Harry and talk with him for a few moments, thank him again for the foot massage? It really had helped.

I shook my head. The hostess going looking for the help? Bad idea. If the paparazzi got wind of that … I didn't know where Becki was, and if she saw me with him, she was sure to tell my father. I counted myself lucky that she hadn't said anything earlier—or had she, and that was why Handsome Harry was conspicuous by his absence? The last thing I wanted to do was upset my father and mess up Amalia's plans … whatever they were.

Grabbing the basket full of cards off the table, I carried it up to my room. The contact lenses were killing me, and I couldn't wait to get those suckers out of my eyes. No matter what else I did to myself, the eye surgery was at the top of the list.

It took me almost an hour to unweave my hair, brush it, and get all the makeup off my face. As I'd expected, I was blotchy, but sleep should help. When I finally dropped into bed, I was out like a light.

* * *

By the time I woke up with a champagne hangover the next morning, it was after eleven. I dragged myself into the bathroom, swallowed two analgesic tablets, and took a shower, shampooing twice to get all the product out of my hair. Unwilling to spend the time it took to dry it, I pulled it back into a low ponytail—all except the dang tendrils that didn't reach. Grabbing two bobby pins, I secured them in place and got dressed. I needed coffee in the same way I needed air.

Wearing jeans, cowboy boots, and a t-shirt that read, *my temper isn't a problem, your stupidity is*, a birthday gift from Antonia, Amalia's thirteen-year-old daughter, I entered the pristine kitchen. Someone must've been up since the wee hours to get this all clean. Unlike my father who still ate in the small dining room, I preferred to have my first meal of the day in there and sat at the butcher block table. The cook stood at the counter.

"Good morning, Maria. I hope there wasn't too big a mess to clean up. That little shindig wasn't my idea. Any chance I can get a cup of coffee?"

"G'Morning to you, Ms. Andressa." She turned to look at me. "There's a fresh pot waiting for you." She pointed to the newspaper on the table. "You're quite the celebrity now, not that you haven't been before, but a prince? Just like Meghan Markle. A fairy tale come true."

I groaned and looked at the picture. It was taken just as we stepped onto the dance floor. I was still smiling. Great. This was far more notoriety than I wanted, and if the prince was Daddy's choice, getting out of that relationship had just gotten harder.

"As for cleaning this mess, I didn't do none of it," she continued. "Them catering people took care of it all. Cleaned the whole house just like that." She snapped her fingers. "That's a mighty fine t-shirt you're wearing. A gift from Tonia?"

"How did you guess?"

She chuckled. "That girl loves those t-shirts with sayings on them."

"That she does."

The aroma of the coffee was reviving me, and when she set a mug down on the table, I inhaled deeply. Since I drank it black, the only successful attempt I'd had at cutting down on fat and sugar, the rich, dark brew didn't need doctoring.

"Want some breakfast? I can scramble some eggs for you, and it won't take but a minute to fry up some bacon."

My stomach heaved slightly at the thought of the heavy meal.

"Don't bother. How about toast and some of that crabapple jelly you made?"

"Coming right up. It was so nice of Mr. Myers to give me and the kitchen staff the evening off with pay. I took my grandkids to the movies."

"Yes, that was considerate of him."

Maybe Amalia was right, and I needed to give Daddy a little more slack on his rope.

"By the way, where is everyone?"

Maria busied herself at the counter.

"Mr. Myers and Mr. Dan left just after nine. They were going into Midland for a meeting, but they'll be back for dinner. Ms. Amalia left about an hour ago. She said that if you asked, she'd see you in your office around one-thirty. As for Mrs. Myers, I assume she's still in bed since I haven't seen hide nor hair of her, and she hasn't called down for anything." She placed the toast on the table in front of me and refilled my coffee mug. "Are you sure that you don't want something else?"

"No, thanks, Maria. This is fine."

I'd just finished my breakfast when the kitchen phone rang. Was her highness Queen Becki demanding breakfast in bed for her and Cecily? Since she and Daddy had separate rooms although they were connected, anything was possible.

Maria walked over to the wall phone and answered. "Yes … She's right here." She turned to me. "It's Jake at the stables."

I frowned, stood, and took the receiver from her. I'd mentioned that I was taking the day off, so whatever reason he had for calling me had to be serious.

"Hey Jake, what's up?"

"I'm sorry to bother you, Doc, but the boys just called in. There's a badly injured three-year-old in the high pasture. Looks like he got into a fight with a big cat. Four of them followed the cat's trail, hoping they can find him and kill him before he does any more damage. The other two are with the horse. He's still alive, but it doesn't look good. They didn't want to do anything without your say-so."

Jim Crocker had called around, claiming he'd seen a mountain lion, but I'd put it down to the moonshine the man consumed. The big cats rarely left the Trans-Pecos area to the south of us, and if there was one up here, he had to be dang hungry to be so far out of his territory. This cat wasn't old and sick, not if he'd come close to killing a horse.

"The horse is about an hour's ride from here on the high pasture," Jake continued. "Dalton claims he's as good as dead, but we've seen you bring them back before. Since we were fixing to bring that herd down later this week, I sent a crew up to get things ready. Being that it's the end of September, never can tell how soon the snows will come. I'm rounding up a dozen men now to go up and move them today. We won't get them all the way back, but we'll do our best. If there's a big cat on the loose, we can't take any chances. What do you want us to do?"

"Give me ten minutes. Saddle Buttercup, she can use a good run. I'm not saying I can save the horse, but I can always try. Oh, and Jake, make sure all the men are packing. If that mountain lion is brave enough to attack an adult herd of horses, he won't hesitate to try and take down a lone horse and rider. Call the cattle ranch and give them a head's up. Their animals are in the lowlands, so they should be safe, but they need to know what's happening. Call the sheriff and the Wildlife Division of Texas Parks and Wildlife. Tell them we'll be dropping off a big cat for a necropsy as soon as we bag it."

I ended the call and turned to Maria. The concern on the woman's face moved me.

"That doesn't sound good. My son-in-law Emilio left for that pasture this morning."

"I'm sure he'll be fine. I'll bet that horse put up one heck of a fight, so that cat's probably licking a few serious wounds." Otherwise, he would've finished the horse. "When Amalia comes back, tell her I had an emergency—don't give anyone the details. When I get home, I'll let them know what's what, but I don't want them worrying about me. I had enough of that last night. Can you fix me a thermos of coffee and something to eat? Looks like I'll miss lunch, but I should be back in time for dinner."

I emptied the last of my coffee and hurried up to my room to use the facilities, get my hat, my Colt 45, my rifle, and my medical bag, hoping I wouldn't need the guns. I was halfway down the stairs when I met Becki coming up, Cecily tucked under her arm as usual. It looked as if she hadn't been in bed after all. She didn't seem at all pleased to see me.

"Where are you going dressed like that? I heard Jackson Hickman is coming over. He has to rush back to Montana tonight to campaign."

Wouldn't he love to know that I was going out hunting cougar?

Becki caught sight of what I carried. "Why have you got your gun and that rifle?"

I swallowed. If anyone was going to make a mountain out of this molehill, it would be her.

"I always carry a gun when I go riding in the back country, you know that. As to why I have it today, there's a sick animal I have to tend to. I am the vet around here, remember? Give my apologies to Jackson and wish him the best with his campaign."

If the man got elected, then the people deserved the incompetent idiot.

She scoffed. "Dr. Cutler did a fine job of looking after things before you came home."

I rolled my eyes. "Sam Cutler was overworked and understaffed. He was only too happy to turn over the care of the animals at the Quaternity ranch to me."

"If you say so." She patted Cecily's head. Be that as it may, he's agreed to keep looking after Cecily."

"And he is welcome to her."

"You need to come down off your high horse, young lady, and learn some respect for your elders," she snarled.

Elder? She was two years older than I was.

Swallowing my annoyance and knowing Jake and the hands were waiting for me, I nodded.

She harrumphed. "Make sure you're back for dinner. Your father has an announcement to make, one you won't want to miss."

Instead of answering, I nodded once more and hurried down the stairs and out of the house. It looked as if Daddy had made his decision, and Amalia and I were too late. What else could go wrong today?

CHAPTER FIVE

By the time I got back to the ranch, the sun had set. I was exhausted and unfit company for man or beast. I should've been hungry, thirsty at least, but even thinking of getting something to eat or drink seemed beyond me. I was fuzzy-headed, sore, and all I wanted was to crawl into bed.

Despite the fact that it was officially autumn, the scorching sun had blazed down with the intensity of a mid-summer day, raising the temperature into the high eighties by early afternoon, making the job of moving the horses more difficult than it would've been on a cool fall day. The wind gusts had stirred up dust and sand but hadn't brought any relief. Because of it, my hat had spent more time dangling down my back than it had on my head, and since I'd forgotten to bring sunscreen, my face and arms were now a glorious shade of crimson.

To make matters worse, I'd finished the coffee Maria had given me by noon, and thirsty as I was, my canteen was empty by two, leaving my mouth dry and sticky. Jake offered me water every now and then, but I drank sparingly. He was working far harder than I was and needed it more. Thankfully, I hadn't felt the urge to go since there was no privacy anywhere.

My 24-hour deodorant had only managed less than half that time, which wasn't unusual in times of high stress, and while at first I'd sweat like a ten-cent hooker in church, by the time we headed back to the ranch, I didn't noticed it at all. Had to be the wind.

After I'd dealt with the badly injured horse, I'd checked all the horses for wounds, finding only one older mare with deep gashes on her flank. The big cat must've come after her, and the young stallion had gone to her defense. Then, I'd helped the wranglers move the animals to a lower pasture near a stream of fresh water, and four men had stayed there to ride shotgun on the herd tonight. Others would replace them in the morning and help move the herd closer to the main pastures. I'd ordered the men tracking the mountain lion to come back in, too. Far too dangerous to do that at night. Others would pick up the trail at dawn.

Sadly, I was unable to save the horse, the damage to his entrails and blood loss too severe. It was a miracle he was still breathing. He'd put up one hell of a fight though, probably saving another animal in the process, and the blood littering the grass around him hadn't all been his. Knowing I was putting him out of his pain and misery, I'd administered the kill shot myself. Then through tear-filled eyes, I'd treated the mare while the men had loaded the carcass onto the wagon for Emilio to drive back to the ranch. One of the hands had led the injured horse back to the stable and returned with a chuckwagon and a cook. After checking on the mare once more, my last act of the day had been to sign the forms for cremation. Since we hadn't killed the mountain lion, we didn't know if the animal had been diseased. We couldn't take a chance on selling the carcass even for dog food.

I sighed as I approached the back door of the house. Maria would be happy to know her son-in-law was safe and sound for tonight at least, but until that cat was eliminated, there was still danger.

I let myself into the house, knowing I was late for supper and Daddy's big announcement. Whoopy-doo. Did I care that he'd just ruined my shot at happiness? At the moment, I was too beat to even do that. Besides, he was probably furious with me. Being late for dinner was a cardinal sin in this house.

I hadn't been able to call in. I had my cell phone with me, but I'd forgotten to charge it, and when I tried to make a call late in the afternoon, it was dead. I'd consoled myself with the fact that Maria would've given Amalia a sanitized version of where I was. Blame it on the champagne. Not wanting to admit to the men that I'd gone out on the range without a viable cell phone, a severe breach of the rules, I'd opted to keep the lapse to myself.

Setting my hat, rifle, side arm, and medical bag down at the base of the stairs, I went into to kitchen to leave the empty thermos on the counter, grateful to see that Maria wasn't there and that the serving girls were too busy to pay me any mind. I hurried toward the dining room to make my apologies, well aware of the fact that I was dusty, dirty, and probably smelled a lot like Lincoln Ford.

Before I could enter, I heard my name uttered in Becki's strident voice. Hearing that vixen disparage me was the last straw.

"You have to do something about Andressa, Wallis. That girl is as rude and inconsiderate as they come. She treats me worse than she treats the help. I'm your wife. I deserve respect. I told her Jackson was coming to see her, but would she change her mind? No. She knew how important this dinner was. I told her myself that you would be making a big announcement before she went off gallivanting with those cowboys, claiming she had to take care of a sick animal."

Amalia spoke up. "Andressa is Quaternity's vet. Looking after the animals is her responsibility. She doesn't have a mean bone in her body, and she most certainly does not go off gallivanting with the wranglers as you put it. We were supposed to meet after lunch. Maria told me she'd had to tend to a sick horse but had planned to be back in time for dinner. If something happened to change her plans, then it had to be important, more important than Daddy's announcement tonight, and if she didn't call in, well I'm certain there's a logical explanation."

Becki harrumphed. "You all do that, jump to her defense as if she's the golden child. Well, she may be blond, but she's no angel. You don't know anything about that girl. None of you do. You think she's little Miss Goody Two Shoes. Well, she isn't. Do you know what she was doing last night when she should've been charming those delightful men your father chose for her? Men who could've done well for Quaternity? She was cavorting with a waiter in the sunroom. I know I should've told you, Wallis, but I handled it myself and reported the man to his superior, warning him not to pay him. Those people need to learn their place."

"You did what?" Dan cried. "Did you see anything inappropriate happening?"

"I saw him putting her shoe on," she defended her actions, proving to me that she'd been spying on me. "And if she took off her shoes, what else did she remove?"

"She probably had sore feet. Did you ever think of that? What you saw was nothing, and to have him fired just laid us open to a wrongful dismissal suit."

Maybe it was the residual champagne headache, the exhaustion, or the agony filling me at the thought of having to marry a man I didn't love, but something exploded inside me. My body grew so hot I feared I might combust on the spot. No longer in control of myself, I burst into the room, filthy dirty, my hair a mess, the tendrils plastered to my sweaty face, and my clothing covered in dried blood and other body fluids. Every ounce of pain, anger, and frustration I'd sat on for the last ten years spewed through me, destroying what little common sense I had left, ready to put my step-mother in her place. Mama had to be rolling in her grave at the thought that the man she'd loved had replaced her with this ... this hussy.

"Why you bitch!"

The words shot out of my mouth, startling everyone at the table. My fury was a storm, a CAT5 hurricane, more destructive than Katrina, Fiona, and Beryl. I was within an arm's reach of Becki, prepared to scratch out her eyes, when Amalia grabbed me.

"Calm down, Andie. She's not worth it."

Calm down? When had the words *calm down* ever had the desired effect on an angry person? There was no calming down now, not even if I tried.

"How dare you speak to me that way." Becki wrinkled her nose. "What have you been doing?

Wrestling with pigs? You're filthy!" Her cheeks were red. "Have you no manners, bursting in on people eating, stinking like a—"

"Dead horse? It happens in my line of work, but it's better than the fetid stench of your perfume. By the way, what is it called? Eau de Corpse Flower?"

The room took on a strange glow, and my voice seemed to come from far away. My heart pounded in my chest, my pulse throbbed in my ears, and my mouth was dry. It was as if I were watching someone else impersonating me. It was strangely liberating. I paused. What had made me so angry? Ah, yes.

"You had him fired? Why? Because he spoke to me, because he had the compassion to understand that I needed a break and shared his with me? Because he helped me put my shoes on my tired feet? You have no right ascribing your lack of morals to me. I told you last night that nothing happened, and unlike you, I know what the truth is. I needed air, and if you'd been forced to listen to those fools all evening, even you would've sought a few minutes of peace. That man worked hard last night, catering to all the so-called rich and famous. He didn't deserve to be punished for what you thought up in your filthy mind. And as for where I was today, I was out trying to save the life of a horse attacked by a mountain lion. I failed." Tears ran down my cheeks. "Was I with the wranglers? Yes. I helped them move the sixty horses we had in the high pasture to safer fields. There are men spending the night out there, risking their lives to protect those horses. So excuse me if I put my job and lives ahead of you."

"Andressa, you've gone too far." My father raised his voice, and it was a red flag to a mad bull.

"Too far? I've gone too far? No, Daddy dearest, it's you who've gone too far. When my mother died, when I needed your love and compassion, instead of grieving with me, you sent me away to suffer alone while you consoled yourself with one bimbo after another, and then when you finally let me come home again where I can do something with my life, you foist four complete idiots on me. I'll give the fifth the benefit of the doubt since he had the decency not to show up. So what's your big announcement? Which of the Freaky Four was the highest bidder? And when's the wedding, or do you even plan to give me a ceremony like my sisters had? Would you prefer to lock me in a room with him until I get pregnant and then pray I give birth to a son? Because a grandson seems to be the only damn thing that matters to you."

"Andressa, you aren't behaving rationally. I'm still your father. You owe me respect and obedience, and since Becki is your step-mother, the rule applies."

"You can go screaming the Fourth Commandment at me all you want, but it won't change a thing. In the eyes of the law and the Myers family trust, I'm an adult now. I will not marry any of the men you tried to foist on me last night. And as for your damn money, I don't want it. And another thing, I will not honor and respect a slut two years older than me because she's a good ride for you."

"Young lady, you will apologize," my father roared.

"Not in this lifetime," I screamed in return. "What will you do if I don't? Send me to bed without supper? Don't bother. I'll do it myself."

I shook off Amalia's hand, raced out of the room, grabbed my gear, and ran up the stairs to my room, slamming the door shut, tears streaming down my cheeks, and my body shaking. I barely made it to the bathroom before spewing the contents of my stomach, what little there was, into the toilet. I leaned my burning forehead on the porcelain and started to shake as the reality of what I'd said and done gripped me.

The room started to spin, and I descended into the hell I'd created for myself.

* * *

When I opened my eyes again, I was in bed. There was someone sitting on the chaise lounge, but it was too dim in the room to see who it was. I moved, my body stiff and sore, and discovered that I was hooked up to an I V bag, the pole holding it a little farther up the head of the bed. Where had that come from? My head ached, and I moaned.

"You're awake," Amalia cried, hurrying to the bedside. "How do you feel?"

"Like I've been run over by a herd of stampeding horses. I had the worst nightmare…"

My sister giggled. "If you're talking about the magnificent hissy fit you threw in the dining room, it wasn't a nightmare. I only wished someone had videoed it. When your mama said you were going to blow, she wasn't kidding. You were glorious in your indignation. The twins agree. Becki needed to be put in her place. We're all tired of her lording it over us even if she is better than Charlotte or Desiree, but that bar was set very low." She reached for a glass on the side of the bed. "The only downside is that you had to be sick to do it. Here.

Drink this. Dr. Zeran says it'll take a few days to replace all the electrolytes you've lost, but you should be fine come Sunday."

I pulled back against the pillow. "Sick? Not COVID I hope. I recall feeling hot … I lost electrolytes? How? When? Surely not because of a tantrum?"

"No silly, you had heatstroke. If I hadn't found you when I did … It seems overindulging in champagne, followed by exertion in the heat, and an inadequate amount of water leaves you severely dehydrated. Plus, you didn't keep your hat on, had no sunscreen with you, and now resemble a well-done lobster, one that will no doubt look like it's shedding within a few days. But don't worry. Aileen is bringing something that will help. Daddy's waiting to talk to you once you're up for a visit—"

"Dear God, no," I cried, interrupting her. "I can't face him, Amalia, I just can't. Even if I don't remember everything I said, what I do recollect is bad enough. The things I said to Becki … she'll probably be using my bed to toilet Cecily for as long as I live here, which probably won't be too long."

She chuckled. "Relax. Everything's fine, and now that you're awake, it's better than fine. When I found you on the bathroom floor, I swear I aged ten years. I thought you were dead. Your breathing was shallow … Don't you ever do that to us again! Now, I can guarantee Daddy isn't going to yell at you, and neither will Becki." She sat on the side of the bed. "After you ran out of the dining room, leaving us all gawking after you, she demanded he make you apologize. He told her to shut up and to get her damn dog away from the table, then he got up and left the room, taking Dan with him."

I groaned and shook my head. "He probably wanted to know how to write me out of the will." A second thought crossed my mind and I smiled. "I would be fine with that. In fact, it would be great. I have a little money in the trust fund Mama left me, enough to help me get started. I could go and get licensed in another state, and…"

"Will you slow down? Why must you always look at the negative side of things? Never mind. That's not why Daddy wanted to talk to Dan. He wanted to make sure that we sent a formal apology for Becki's behavior to the company and make sure the waiter was compensated for his work." She shook her head. "That was the first time we worked with Ray ... Ray's catering. They did a great job, and we didn't want Becki's elitist attitude and rudeness to ruin our chances of using them again. If you say nothing happened between you and the waiter, I believe you, but you sure did get your dander up over it."

I chewed my bottom lip, stopping when the action caused me pain. My lips were swollen and blistered. Dang sunburn. Best to stay away from people for a day or two. Of course, if my intended saw me like this, he might back out of the deal. Was it worth a shot? Maybe, but then Daddy would just move on to option number two.

Amalia was staring at me. What had she asked? My mind was still a little fuzzy. Something about my getting angry over Handsome Harry. He'd been the spark that had led to the explosion.

"I did, didn't I?" I admitted. "I guess I was beyond reason at that point. Maybe fever? Nothing happened between us, at least nothing she conjured up in her dirty, little mind." Het filled my cheeks, but as red as they were, Amalia wouldn't notice. "All he did was rub my sore feet and then help me with those dang shoes, which I intend never to wear again."

Amalia laughed. "You're kidding."

"I wish I were. He's the nicest man I've ever met."

She narrowed her eyes. "Do tell."

"I went out there to get away from Leopold, and I took off my shoes to give my feet a rest. I didn't know it was the staff respite area. He came in for his break, and he was going to leave when he saw me … anyway, I was searching for my shoes under the chair, ready to leave myself when he found them. He asked me if my feet were sore, I said yes, since I wasn't used to the shoes. He knelt down and massaged them, like he used to do for his grandmother. Amalia, I was ten steps from heaven it felt so good. He slipped my shoes on for me, and that's when Becki burst in, although why she was there was a mystery unless she was spying on me. The woman was insufferably rude to him and to me. He left. I called her on it, and she went on about deserving respect. A few minutes later, after telling her that the last thing I wanted was motherly advice from her, I walked out. That's all there was to it. He was a very nice man, and he was treated badly because he was kind to me."

Amalia touched my hand. "A man who gives foot massages is a treasure indeed. Don't worry. He'll be well-compensated."

"I suppose, but it should never have happened in the first place. Harry didn't deserve that. No one does."

She cocked her head, her eyes wide, her eyebrows burying themselves under her bangs.

"His name was Harry?"

I giggled. "I don't know what it was. I just thought of him as Handsome Harry because he was movie-star gorgeous—at least when compared to the Freaky Four."

Amalia smiled. "That makes sense. Come on. I'll help you to the bathroom to clean up and put on a fresh nightie. Then, we'll get you sitting down so that you can eat while they change the bed. We can't offer you much. You're on a liquid diet, so I'm talking broth, Jello, watermelon cubes, and clear tea, not the sweet stuff either."

"Sounds heavenly, and so does a trip to the bathroom."

She stood, opened the drapes to allow more light into the room, and pulled back the covers. I sat on the side of the bed, surprised by how weak I felt. When I thought I could stand, I did and leaned heavily on her as she pushed the I V pole while I struggled with the twenty slow steps to the bathroom. After I'd used the toilet, washed my hands and face, put on the clean nightie waiting for me on the hook, brushed my tangled hair, and cleaned my teeth, I was beat. Opening the door, I pushed my walking buddy out ahead of me, let her lead me to an easy chair that hadn't been in my room earlier, and settle me in it with a lap quilt covering my legs and feet. I was as weak as a newborn baby. She pushed a tray table over to me.

I looked around the room, noticing more chairs.

"Where did all this come from?"

"Daddy ordered it to make it easier for us. Someone's stayed by your side ever since the collapse."

"Why? Heatstroke can be dangerous, but…"

She put up her hand to silence me. "Andie, we were all worried about you. When I found you, you were burning up and scarcely breathing. I went screaming through the house … It was a big relief when the doctor diagnosed sunstroke. Daddy was afraid … he thought he'd pushed you too far and that you might've taken something from your medical bag."

I straightened myself in the chair. "You know that I would never do that."

"I know, but Becki was screaming that you'd lost your mind and were obviously high on something. Daddy called Dr. Zeran, and he was here with his nurse in no time. He checked you over, and then when he was sure you hadn't hurt your neck or your back, he made me and the nurse help you into the tub and fill it with cold water to bring down your fever. You were shivering so badly, but you still didn't wake up. Daddy lifted you out of the bath himself—wouldn't let anyone else touch you. The nurse and I undressed you and dried you off. I got you a nightgown and then, after we wrapped you in blankets to stop the shuddering, he carried you to bed. The doctor gave you a needle to stop the quaking, the nurse put in a catheter and hooked up the IV. When your urine output was deemed normal earlier this afternoon, she took out the catheter and stopped the meds. As for Becki, she's not here. He had the doctor sedate her, and in the morning he sent her to a spa in Dallas. If you ask me, it's a rehab center. She'll be there for another week at least. That woman has a drinking problem."

"You think?" I straightened suddenly as other thoughts raced through my mind. "Oh my God! The horses. The mare. They'll have to have someone call Dr. Cutler to look at her. She'll need antibiotics and those claw marks kept clean." I licked my lips. "Have they found the mountain lion?"

"Relax. It's all under control. The horses are in the west pasture, safe and sound. Doc Cutler has seen to the mare, and she's fine. Good thing, too, because she's pregnant. As for the cat, they found him in a box canyon, but he was already dead. That horse gave as good as he got. The necropsy showed all kinds of internal damage but no disease."

I scowled. "Necropsy? Already?"

"Andie, it's Thursday. You've slept the last three days and most of this one."

I gasped, my eyes opening wide, my jaw dropping. Almost four days? How could I have slept all that time? I'd been tired and emotionally overwrought, but four days? I couldn't recall ever being sick enough to do that!

"You're kidding," I whispered, unable to grasp the reality of it.

She shook her head and patted my hand.

"Dr. Zeran felt it was best to keep you sedated. He doesn't think there's any organ damage, but it's always a possibility. Don't worry about it now. I'll go down and tell the nurse, Maria, Daddy, and the twins that you're awake. He'll be relieved. He's been haunting your room at all hours. He hasn't left the house since I went screaming into the study, telling them I'd found you passed out on the floor."

"I'm sorry I scared ya'll. I wasn't thinking clearly. I was upset about that fool article in the newspaper. You know how I loathe publicity and that idiot headline … Then, Jake called about the horse … My mind was elsewhere. I know better than to go out without water and sunscreen."

She reddened and looked away.

What was she keeping from me?

"What?" I demanded, eyes narrowed.

Shaking her head, she smiled. "It's nothing. Forget it. You didn't do it purposely. Besides, something good came from it."

"You mean other than the fact that I delayed the inevitable, the knowledge of which of the Freaky Four won the auction?"

"Yes, silly, and you've got to stop being negative. None of them won the auction as you call it." She grabbed my hand. "Andie, you did it. You earned your freedom—well, at least for a year. I'll let Daddy tell you all about it." She laughed. "He actually thinks it's his idea."

My mouth dropped open as I watched her leave the room.

A few moments later, the door opened, and Maria entered with Lucy, one of the servants, and a redheaded woman in mint green scrubs. Maria set down the tray she carried on the desk, while Lucy hurried over to strip the bed and remake it.

The woman carried a small medical bag.

"Hello, Dr. Myers. I'm Cathy, Dr. Zeran's nurse. You gave your family quite the scare. Let me check you over."

She removed several pieces of medical equipment from the bag. Using a flashlight, she checked my pupil response. She used her stethoscope to examine my heart, my lungs, and my breathing, took my temperature, and finally my pulse, and my blood pressure.

Smiling, she repacked her bag.

"Your fever's gone, your eyes are clear and bright, and your vitals are all normal. Mrs. Steele said you used the lavatory, so I can remove this." She pointed to the I V. Within seconds, she had the needle out of my arm and a band-aid in place. "Just remember to drink as much as you can. I'll call the doctor. He'll want to see you for himself before we make any more changes, but I'd say you were well on your way to recovery. Now, I'll let Maria give you something to eat, and when you finish, the family can join you for a little while. You need your rest."

I laughed. "Rest? I've been asleep for four days. How much rest do I need?"

"Dr. Myers, do I really have to answer that? You know the dangers of heatstroke as well as I do. You're on the mend, but it can take your body months to recover completely. You'll have to watch yourself. Your father was furious that someone leaked your condition to the press, but Dr. Zeran gave a statement, and because of it, the health authorities were able to put out valuable information about the dangers of sunstroke. No one thinks of it at this time of the year, but as you learned, it's a serious problem. Your mishap may well save lives. Now, please eat."

With that, she left the room.

Knowing Maria's weakness for newspaper gossip, I turned to her.

"What leaked article?"

The housekeeper shook her head.

"It wasn't anything bad. They had a picture of you riding without a hat. Must've been taken from a distance. Probably one of those paparazzi your father has chased off the ranch every now and then. The headline made me laugh. 'Heiress princess collapses after riding without her crown.' Now, don't fret none."

Not fret? How could I not be upset? My carelessness out there for the world to see? The last thing I wanted was more publicity.

She placed the tray in front of me.

"Eat it all, ya hear. I'm not leaving this room until you do."

"Yes, ma'am." There was no point in getting angry with her. "Maria, do you know who might've leaked the story to the press?"

She continued tidying the room as I ate. Was she avoiding giving me an answer? It certainly seemed like it.

"Maria?"

She stopped and looked at me.

"The only one who wasn't busy helping you was Mrs. Myers. After your father spoke to her, she was as mad as a wet hen." She shrugged. "Could've been her."

I nodded. It was certainly possible, but what would she hope to gain from it?

CHAPTER SIX

Still fuming over what I saw as another of Becki's betrayals, I pushed the tray away.

"I can't eat any more." I'd consumed more than two-thirds of its contents. "But I'll keep the mint tea."

Maria smiled. "You done well, Ms. Andressa. You'll be fit as a fiddle in no time."

She picked up the tray and left the room. Glancing outside, through the open curtains beside me, I could see night had fallen. It still amazed me that so much time had passed, time I could've used to plot my escape from Daddy's decision— whatever it had been. Now … Could I use my illness to buy me time? As Cathy had said, heatstroke was no laughing matter. I could've died or suffered permanent organ damage. The reality was sobering.

I'd just set down the empty tea cup when the door opened a crack.

"Okay if we come in now?" Amalia's face filled the gap.

"Yes, please."

No time like the present to face the dragon. Besides, if it got bad, I could plead exhaustion and ask everyone to leave.

Daddy, Alison, Aileen, and Amalia entered the room.

"You look so much better." Aileen stepped over to the chair and bussed my cheek. "I brought some aloe vera gel for your skin and medicated lip balm." She settled in the chair near me.

Alison stepped over and kissed my cheek.

"Aileen's right. You look better than when I saw you earlier this morning. I filled that prescription the doctor left for the electrolyte powder. I gave it to Maria. You had us worried, cupcake." She settled on a chair next to Aileen.

"I told you. Nothing can keep a good woman down for long," Amalia added, dragging a chair over to sit beside me.

My father stood in front of me. He looked tired, almost haggard as if he hadn't slept in days.

He cleared his throat. "Andressa, you frightened me girl, I'll admit that, but it made me realize that I haven't been the kind of father that Anya wanted me to be. I'm sorry for that, but from here on, I plan to do better. I loved your mother deeply, and while you may not believe it, losing her was the worst thing that ever happened to me—until I thought I'd lost you. Dr. Zeran says you need time to rest and fully recover. I thought you could do it here … I mean Quaternity has everything you could possibly want, but Alison said it would never work because you would want to look after the animals, and as always, she's right. I heard you asked about them, so they would definitely be on your mind. Amalia mentioned a retreat and spa on Santa

Catalina Island, a quiet place in the hills. All of your sisters have gone there at one time or another. People stay for days, weeks, even months. She mentioned that you haven't painted in years. You used to be good at it. Maybe there, away from everything, you could start again. That's why I would like you to consider going there. It's your decision … you deserve that much. Go to Shangri-la, the island retreat. Rest, relax, and center yourself as they say. Then, once you're rested and refreshed, if you feel up to it, perhaps you'd like to travel. You've got a passport, but you've only used it to go to Mexico. There's a whole other world out there." He rubbed the back of his neck. "Australia has some of the world's top grassfed cattle ranches. I attended the Melbourne Cup a few years ago with your mother. Those horses were impressive. You might be interested in checking out their breeding system. "I've been in touch with a couple of owners who may be willing to part with stock. At any rate, Dan will see to it that whatever safety measures needed are in place. I want you to be happy, Andie. It's all I ever wanted."

"That's kind of you, Daddy," I mumbled, surprised by the use of Mama's nickname for me and trying to ignore the excitement on my sisters' faces. A retreat on Catalina? I'd never heard of that. "What about my … my wedding?" Amalia had said he hadn't picked one but that didn't mean he wasn't planning to do so.

He chuckled, somewhat embarrassed. "We can let that go for now. Observing those men the other night, it seems I didn't choose well. Your sisters were rather vocal about that. I assume you agree?"

I nodded. Could it be that simple?

"You missed my announcement at dinner Sunday evening. I've decided it's time I stepped back a bit. Anderson will be picking up the reins of the company. I'll be there as an advisor if he needs me, but I'm not getting any younger. When Becki gets back, we're going on an around the world cruise since we really didn't have a honeymoon. I'll make sure she understands her position in this family. You and your sisters come first." He cleared his throat. "And as for a grandson, well, an old man can dream, but if you give me another grand-daughter, I'll love her as much as I do the magnificent seven. When we return to the ranch, with Anderson's help, I'll put together a more favorable group. And if you don't like one of them, we'll try again. I take my responsibilities as a father and the vow I made your mother seriously. You don't have to worry about anything. Sam Cutler has an assistant who's quite capable of looking after the livestock for a year. Now, I'd best let the rest of the staff know that you're fine and will be away for a while. Amalia has made all of the arrangements." He turned to her. "When does she leave?"

Amalia stood. "On Sunday morning. Dr. Zeran said she'll be able to travel by then. We're using the company jet and hope to leave at ten. You'll have time to say goodbye before you leave for Dallas."

"Excellent."

He came around the bed, bent down, and kissed my forehead.

I couldn't recall the last time he'd done that.

"I'm very glad you're going to be all right. I may not always show it, but I love you."

I couldn't remember when he'd actually said those words, and in my frail state, I fought to keep the tears back.

"I love you, too, Daddy," I mumbled gruffly.

He smiled and nodded. "So, will you go to this retreat? The choice is yours."

I nodded. "Yes, and thank you for … for everything."

"It's the least I can do as your sisters were quick to point out. Now, I have quite a bit of paperwork to attend to which I've neglected. I'll leave you to gossip with them, but only until nine. You need your rest."

"Yes, Daddy," they answered as one.

As soon as he closed the door, Amalia approached the bed.

I immediately broached the topic of the paparazzi picture and story Cathy had mentioned, examining their faces closely as I spoke.

"Maria thinks it was Becki,' I finished.

"If she *is* the one who did it," Aileen stated, "Then, she'd done you a great service. It made it easier for us to convince Daddy you needed time—a lot of time—away from here. Of course, heatstroke wasn't what I had in mind, and I'm so relieve that you're going to be fine—we all are."

"Thanks. Now tell me about this retreat on Catalina. I don't recall any of you mentioning it. How long do I really have to stay there? You know I had something else in mind, but painting again doesn't sound half bad. I did miss it, but I was so busy with school and then there was starting my practice here and the horse."

Alison pushed her short hair off her face. "Actually, none of us have been there."

I frowned. "But daddy said—"

Amalia sat beside me once more. "Ingrid said you would have to stay three months, four tops."

My scowl deepened with my confusion. "Ingrid? My Ingrid?"

"Yes. I spoke to her Sunday morning after the party. I needed her advice. I had a plan to get you away … As it turned out, she had the perfect solution. She and Will have opened a clinic in the mountains last winter for their more exclusive patients. I told her what you want done, and that's the timeline to be fully healed. After that, you'll come back to LA and put the second part of your plan in play. Richard's sister, Kelly, works with a placement agency. She'll help you as much as she can and has a friend who works for one of the studios who can get you passable ID under an assumed name. Once you have a job, she'll help you get a place to stay. I've always wanted to visit Australia, so Dan and I will make a second honeymoon of it and look over the cattle and horses. The rest will be up to you."

Tears filled my eyes. "You guys … I don't know how to thank you."

Alison smiled. "Thank us by following your dream. All we want is for you to be happy."

* * *

Four months later

Dressed in my bra and panties, I stood in front of the full-length mirror in Will Jordan's consultation room, hardly able to believe the reflection was mine. He'd given me my last checkup, had explained what I needed to keep doing, and had provided me with the creams he recommended, including a powerful sunscreen. I was good to go. In some ways, I was sorry to be leaving here. It had been wonderful spending time with Ingrid again.

The procedures and the respite I'd gotten had helped me come to grips with so many aspects of who and what I was, aiding me to understand that all of my misery and lack of confidence hadn't only been about my appearance. It had been about grieving my mother, something I'd never done properly. Added to that had been a deep-seated sense of abandonment and the fear of loving someone and losing them again that had made me keep everyone including my family at arm's length. In Will's words, I'd needed to feel beautiful on the outside to see the beautiful me on the inside.

Whatever it was, it had worked, and armed with a new confidence, it was time to face the world and move on to stage two of my plans. After all, I only had eight months left, not a lot of time to live with my new face and body and find the man who would be the right fit for me. Handsome Harry showed up in my dreams now and then, but he and I could never make it work. He knew who I was, and even if by some miracle we met again and fell in love, I would never know if it was with me or my money.

Since clinic policy dictated that patients weren't allowed to see themselves until the transformation was complete, this was the first time I'd seen all of me. I'd not only lost those stubborn twenty pounds, but I was also fit and toned. My new bra was a 34DD, the average bust size for an American woman, a modest bust compared to some of the Hollywood starlets and Beverly Hills' wives who were here for procedures of their own. But it was my face that was most startling. As Amalia had predicted, I resembled my mother, but my sapphire eyes were larger and brighter than hers had ever been.

Even knowing what I'd planned to do the morning Amalia and I had left the ranch, I would never have expected it to turn out this way. Not only did I look like a new woman, I also felt like one.

By the time we'd arrived at Shangri-la that Sunday afternoon, I was exhausted. Ingrid had examined me and dictated that I was to go straight to bed. Her husband, Will Jordan, would examine me in the morning, and I'd be given my schedule for surgery. Agnes Parker, the dietician would be in later, and my transformation as they referred to the procedures I was scheduled to undergo would begin. The last thing she did before leaving me alone with my sister to unpack was request that any mirrors I had, and my cell phone go back with

Amalia. The resort had a private line I could use once a week to check in with family.

When Amalia complained that this sounded more like an indoctrination facility than a spa retreat, Ingrid explained that the ability to unplug and be unavailable was as crucial to my treatment as the surgery, diet, exercise, art therapy, and whatever other interests I opted to pursue.

"Will believes in treating the whole patient— body and soul. We need our patients to trust us completely, surrender themselves to us so that we can do our best for them." She chuckled. "Don't worry. Will has never had a dissatisfied client. Besides, Andressa is a friend."

Reluctantly, I agreed, promising to contact Amalia every Sunday evening. She would pass on the *rules* to Daddy so that he wouldn't be upset if he called my cell phone, and I didn't answer.

When I met Will the following day, he gave me a thorough physical examination, before focusing on my face. He would do a peel to remove the skin damaged by the sunburn, reminding me that after the procedures were complete, I was to avoid going out in the sun without sunscreen. Then, we discussed my chest, or rather my lack of one. I explained what I wanted. Satisfied that I knew my own mind, he showed me pictures of eyelifts, chin remodeling, smaller noses as well as augmentations. He was quite pleased with all my choices.

Next came the dietician who went through my food preferences, explaining how she planned to cure my carb addiction—not that I believed that was even possible. She was followed by the trainer who designed a physical fitness program for me, one I would have no trouble keeping up with for the rest of my life. I went through aerobic exercises three mornings a week, and did weight training the other three with Sunday as a day of rest. Once my stitches were healed, I swam every morning, hiked through the woods on clear days, or used the treadmill and exercise bike on others. I couldn't ride here, but once I was able to, I would add that to my routine.

In the afternoons, I painted, took a class, or sat in on wellness seminars. I made friends with Ursula, no last names here. She was a producer's prodigy sent here to work off the flab as she put it, get killer jugs, and hone up on her diction—in her case a Texas accent. After all the years I'd spent in upstate New York, my accent had waned, so I enjoyed talking to her and listening to the familiar sounds and expressions of home. Once she'd finished her program and left Shangri-la, I'd taken a course in mixology, the art of mixing and creating drinks. The cocktails I made were alcohol-free, but I loved combining the various ingredients. My mojito won first prize in our bartending tournament at the end of the course. I received a small trophy and a certificate of completion that was college certified. When I mentioned that to Amalia on my weekly call, she promised to let Kelly know for the job search. Working in a bar was a sure way to meet men of all ilks.

On the third day, the hairdresser had examined my hair and discussed it with both Will and Ingrid.

The next thing I knew, she'd cut it to the same length as the wayward tendrils—chin length—and had given me a color lift turning my Scandinavian white-blond hair that washed me out to an acceptable California golden-blond. I had to admit it was cooler and far easier to wash than my long hair had been. Besides, it was the one change that wasn't meant to be permanent.

The following day, a laser eye surgeon had corrected my myopia, eliminating the need for glasses and contact lenses. It had been uncomfortable for a few days, my exercise routine moderated, but by the time Will was ready to work his magic, I could see better than I ever had even with my rose-tinted glasses.

The first thing he'd done was the augmentation which hurt far more than I'd expected it to. The next week, he'd dealt with the congenital ptosis, the droopy upper eyelids, giving me normal eyelids for the first time in my life, and allowing me to see without what sometimes felt like a heavy curtain waiting to descend. Once that surgery was deemed healing, he went to work on the rest of my face. He shortened, straightened, and narrowed my large, slightly crooked nose and sculpted my jaw so that it no longer receded.

The door opened, and I reached for the sheet to cover myself, not that I expected a stranger to walk in.

Ingrid grinned.

"Will's done some fantastic work in the past, but you're his masterpiece. It's been hard not seeing how you looked, but had you seen yourself all bruised and swollen … it wouldn't have helped. In fact, you would've felt worse than you did when you arrived. What do you think?"

I smiled, admiring my new bosom, nothing overblown, and it fit perfectly on my toned body.

"I love it. I look like … like my mother. Honestly, Ingrid, it couldn't be more perfect." I threw my arms around her, careful not to squash her pregnant belly.

She smiled. "That's what I like to hear. Now, just because your procedures are over, it doesn't mean you can't come back. A lot of our patients return and stay here for a few days or weeks just to relax and ground themselves. Even with a beautiful face, things aren't always easy out there. A lot of the baggage weighing you down when you got here is waiting for you when you leave, and the paparazzi has been searching for you for months. There was another missing heiress headline with an old picture at the grocer's this morning."

"Dang! I was hoping I was no longer the flavor of the month. Amalia mentioned one guy who keeps coming around the ranch, but since I have no intention of going there just yet—"

I stopped talking. I'd agreed to keep my plans secret from everyone, including Ingrid.

"Well, when they find you and comment on your new beauty, don't forget to put in a good word for Will." She rubbed her lower back. "If you aren't going back to the ranch and your practice, where are you going?"

"I'm going to travel, see something of the world."

Ingrid nodded. "That's great. Traveling is a wonderful way to meet new people and come out of your shell. I'm hoping you'll come for a visit after the baby's born. But enough of this and long goodbyes. It's really just a *see you soon*. Your plane landed so I expect whichever sister is coming to get you will be here soon. Let's get you back to your room and dressed. All your new clothes have arrived, and those you came with will be divided among several women's shelters as you requested. I'm certain that if you want anything dressier, you can find it on Rodeo Drive, or in London, Paris, or Rome. I envy you. I wanted to go to Europe this year for our vacation, but with the baby…" She shrugged. "Next year for sure."

"Definitely, and as for the clothing, you're right," I agreed, although I doubted I would. The jeans, slacks, shorts, skirts, sundresses, t-shirts, and blouses I'd ordered from the shop on the island that serviced the clinic would be fine for now.

"Then, since my bladder is demanding to be emptied, I'll let you get dressed." She headed toward the door. "I'll see you before you leave."

I put on the robe I'd worn earlier and hurried to my room.

Twenty minutes later, dressed in the skinniest jeans I'd ever owned, a midriff-baring top, and my cowboy boots, I was closing my suitcase when someone knocked on the door.

Thinking it was the porter here for my luggage which consisted of several completed, wrapped paintings and my suitcase, I reached for my purse and called, "Come in."

The door opened, and a gasp arose from the three women standing in the doorway.

"Andressa?"

Feeling a little foolish, I nodded.

"My God," Alison exclaimed. "You look just like your mother."

"You do," Aileen added, "Only I can see the old you in the way you carry yourself, but sister, you are going to set the world on fire."

"Wow. I knew you'd look like her, but it's everything, the body, the hair, the face, and the eyes." Amalia's smile couldn't be any wider without damaging her face. "Without the droopy lids, they just pop. I never realized what a gorgeous color they were. I can't wait to see what happens when he sees you."

"Who? Daddy?"

"Yes, of course Daddy. Who else?" she answered too quickly. "Aileen, don't you have news for Andie?"

Aileen frowned, looked at her, and then nodded.

"Of course I do. I thought we were saving it for the ride to LA." She smiled at me. "Kelly found you a great job. There's this little comedy club in East LA owned by an old friend of hers. He lost his wife a few months ago. They ran the place together, but he can't keep it up alone so he's looking for a new bartender. She suggested you, and he's agreed to see you on Monday. If he likes what he sees, the job is yours. The place is called The Pickleback, named after its signature drink. It's a little kitschy, so it won't attract the kind of people you're dead-set on avoiding. To my mind, it's exactly what you're looking for. She'll take you to see some apartments tomorrow—oh, and you have a new identity. Andie Harper, a cowgirl from Texas, come to LA to see the sights. With false identities, it's always easiest to stick to the truth as much as you can."

I nodded. "That makes sense, and I'm less likely to get tripped up. I was helping out a friend and polishing my Texan. Looks like I'll get to use it, too."

A man cleared his throat. "Excuse me. I was sent to get the bags."

I smiled. "Yup. All of that, please." I pointed to the pile of paintings and turned to my sisters. "There's one for each of you and another for Daddy. I hope ya'll will like them. Now, let's get this here wagon train moving."

Amalia smiled. "I'm going to like this new, confident, version of you."

I grinned. "Me, too."

Now, all I had to do was make it happen.

* * *

Five months later

By mid-June, I'd entrenched myself in California culture and had experienced almost everything I'd ever hoped to do. I'd walked along the beach at sunset, had gone shopping at funky boutiques, and had eaten street meat while sitting by my easel, drawing caricatures of the people I saw. I'd even sold a few. One day, when the truth of my adventures surfaced, those ten-dollar drawings might be worth a lot more. To date, my favorite artistic endeavor was the painting of a sunset off Venice Beach. That watercolor hung in the small living room of the apartment I rented from Veronica Richards, a retired police officer. The place was in a family-oriented neighborhood and was as safe as any in that section of LA. After all, a bartender couldn't very well live in Beverly Hills.

Being plain, old Andie Harper was liberating—well, maybe not plain or old—but I fit in and was as comfortable with the people I met as I'd been with the wranglers, cowboys, and staff back home. No one expected anything from me other than a smile and their favorite drink. I didn't have personal security following me around, paparazzi clamoring for my picture, and no one stared at the flat-chested troll. That shy, self-conscious girl was gone, replaced by one who smiled a lot, had learned to flirt, and had developed a quick wit.

Unfortunately, some relentless paparazzi, unaware of the truth, continued to decorate the tabloids with one made-up story after another. The yellow journalist who'd rarely paid any attention to me were obsessed with the missing heiress. Each week, when I did my groceries, I picked up a copy of the local rag. The stories were creative if completely devoid of facts. One had claimed my heatstroke had been so severe that it had cause brain damage and that I was now confined to a wheelchair and would be living out my life in a private hospital. The article had even had an AI generated photo of me sitting in a garden with a nurse by my side. Another had claimed I was being held prisoner by some militant environmentalists who demanded that Quaternity cease oil production if they ever wanted to see me alive again. A third had me refusing to marry Prince Leopold and being sent to a convent until I agreed. Little did the writer know how close he'd come to the truth. I had indeed refused to marry the prince. My personal favorite was the one that claimed my longtime addiction to drugs had been exacerbated by my illness and that I'd run away from the ranch to live in a commune in Mexico. At times, their imaginations were quite creative. If I had a say in the matter, I would suggest they quit journalism and write screenplays for Spanish telenovela episodes. They'd make a fortune.

I continued to check in with Amalia each Sunday, discussing my success at finding Mr. Right, or rather my lack of it. After touring the Far East and Australia earlier, Daddy was now on a South

American and Antarctic tour, having the time of his life. He'd loved seeing Brazil again, not having returned since my mother's death. I wasn't sure how much fun Becki was having since her name hadn't come up, but in all honesty, I didn't care.

While there were several things weighing on my mind, my job wasn't one of them. Working behind the bar at The Pickleback was more satisfying and rewarding than anything I'd imagined. I'd known from the start that it was only temporary, and while I loved being a veterinarian, there was a lot of satisfaction in just making people happy for a few hours. I slung beer, mixed drinks, drew caricatures of the acts, and had polished my sense of humor, since part of my job involved introducing the comedians.

The only fly in the ointment was time. I had less than three months left to find the man of my dreams, the man who would love me for me. Not having had a lot of experience dating, other than a few rich boys in college, one of whom had taken my virginity and then dumped me, I wasn't the best judge of character. Still, I'd had fun, but none of the men I'd dated had affected me the way Handsome Harry had at my birthday.

CHAPTER SEVEN

When it was time for me to leave The Pickleback, I would miss it. The bar was named after a drink that consisted of a shot of Irish whiskey, usually Jameson, followed by an ounce of pickle juice or a bite from a dill pickle. Since the bar owner's name was Jack Daniels, he'd opted to replace the Irish with the good old Tennessee whiskey he claimed as his namesake.

Naming the bar after its signature drink wasn't much of a stretch. With its eclectic décor that had something in it from just about everywhere and every beer and liquor company known to man, the place was both fascinating and trashy. After working here for five months, I could still discover something new each day. It was like playing *Where's Waldo?* but on a larger scale.

While the floor, tables, chairs, and the bar were cleaned daily, I couldn't say the same for the many knickknacks and gadgets on the high shelves or hanging from the walls and ceiling. Earl, the stuffed elk's head above the bar, boasted cobwebs between his antlers, and Lord alone knew what other creatures might've settled in there.

I doubted there was an undecorated inch in the place. Yet, come any holiday, they managed to add more. I'd seen pictures of the place. Halloween saw spider webs and spiders joining ranks with pumpkins, skeletons, bats, and icky, green-faced witches. Those were followed by pilgrim hats and paper turkeys for Thanksgiving. Santa, pine trees, and artificial snow appeared for Christmas, when they hung balls from the mortified animal's antlers along with Happy New Year signs. Thankfully, those vanished a few weeks later to be replaced with Valentine's Day hearts and cupids. I'd started work a week before St Patrick's Day with its shamrocks and shillelaghs. Those had given way to bunnies and colored eggs for Easter. In May, the place had hosted a Cinco de Mayo party, with sombreros and chili peppers, and I'd created a Pickleback marguerita for the occasion. There would soon be red, white and blue bunting around along with Stars and Stripes to celebrate the Fourth of July. Yup. I was definitely going to miss it here.

I sobered, reminded once more that I was almost out of time. He was out there, I was certain of it, but where?

It had taken me a while to get comfortable with the customers hitting on me—both male and female—and the leers and wolf whistles I got when I stepped out on stage, but eventually it had dawned on me that their attention was exactly what I wanted. I used it to my advantage. If someone's eyes were focused on my tits and ass, they weren't likely to recognize my face, not that it was recognizable now. Each week, someone left a tabloid on the bar. So far, no one had made the connection between the hot bartender and the troll. Will's bill for services had been astronomical but worth every cent.

I continued cutting fruit for tonight's cocktails, getting the bar ready for the Friday-after-work crowd.

"Andie, you got a minute?"

My boss, the bar's owner, sat on a stool at the end of the bar. From the look on his face, he had news to deliver, news my gut told me I wasn't going to like. Was he firing me? It was true business had dropped, but it would pick up again come July.

"Sure'nuff, Jack." I'd learned to play up my Texan accent, something else the bar patrons found quaint. "Ain't expecting anyone for another fifteen-twenty minutes. Kin I get you anything?"

"Just coffee."

I poured him a cup, added the two spoonfuls of sugar he liked, and enough cream to lighten it.

"Here you go. Now, you look like there's a burr under your saddle. What did you want to speak to me about?"

"I wanted you to be the first to know. I sold The Pickleback, Andie."

My knees buckled.

"You did what?" I squeaked, grabbing the edge of the bar before I collapsed and wishing I'd poured myself a stiff drink.

"I sold the bar. The real estate guy who's in charge of the neighborhood gentrification project around here brought me a bona fide offer from a big entertainment consortium, the ones building the hotel next door."

The air whooshed out of me. I'd seen the sign on the outside of the boards protecting the construction site. Rayburn Enterprises.

"They offered me more than twice what the place is worth," he continued. "Long range plans are to amalgamate it into the hotel. Not sure they'll keep the name but…" He frowned. "Andie, are you alright? You look like you've seen a ghost."

A ghost? Not exactly, but a demon from the past? Definitely. Cole Rayburn. I'd forgotten all about the man who'd been behind door number five in the Marriage Sweepstakes. Had Daddy crossed him off the list of eligible men like the rest of the Freaky Four? He hadn't bothered to come to my birthday party—well, to be fair it hadn't been his fault—but suddenly, here was his specter about to ruin my life as surely as he would have if he had been there that night.

Trying to pull myself together, I grabbed the tabloid someone had left on the bar and tossed it into the trashcan, my eyes glimpsing the headline on the front page. *Missing Heiress seen in Norway.*

Seriously? Another example of the Yellow Press making up the news instead of reporting it, although I had planned to visit all of Scandinavia someday.

"Andie, I asked you if you were okay." Jack's voice betrayed his concern. "You're as white as your blouse."

I'd worn white the night of my birthday, too.
The dang color didn't even suit me, but each time I
wore it, bad things happened. That t-shirt I'd worn
the day I'd had to put down the horse had been
white, too … at least it had started out that way. The
blouse I wore now was part of the outfit I'd chosen
to wear while tending the bar—white blouse, black
loose trousers held up by black suspenders that
framed my bust, emphasizing it, and a man's red tie
worn in a large, floppy bow, the tie ends floating
just above my chest. It worked both behind the bar
and when I had to go onstage, although how long I
would be doing either was a mystery.

I shook my head. "Low blood sugar. I forgot to
eat lunch today." I poured myself half a glass of
coke and guzzled it, letting out a loud, unladylike
burp. "Sorry 'bout that." I crinkled my brow. "I
don't understand, Jack. You love this place."

"Honey, I just can't do this anymore. I almost
locked the doors and walked away until Kelly told
me she had someone who could help me out, and
you've been damn good for this place, but the

offer's just too good to pass up. Eventually, they would've opened their own bar in the hotel, and I would've gone belly-up, with nothing to show for all the years we put into it. This way, I'm walking away with enough to guarantee a bright future for my grandchildren. The Pickleback was Luella's dream, and with her gone ... I'm tired. They'll be closing down for a few weeks while they renovate, but they're giving all the staff vacation pay to make up for it. They'll be up and running again by Labor Day. They gave me their word. Your job here is safe for as long as you want it. I made sure of that."

I shook my head. Labor Day? I wouldn't be staying much past that. My year would be up, and I was dang sure Daddy wouldn't give me an extension. As much as I'd come to love Jack, he was more naïve than any business owner I'd ever met—and believe me, I'd met plenty. Once the documents were signed, anything not in writing wouldn't be worth a plug nickel. If this was a dream, it was the mother of all nightmares.

"I'm not sure you should trust the word of a conglomerate like that. More than likely, they're just going to tear the place down and fling us all out on our ears."

"That's not going to happen. Let me tell you what the lawyer I spoke to told me a short while ago. Rayburn Enterprises is under new management. When the old man retired, the new CEO, Cole Rayburn, decided that it was time to start thinking about others, not just the company's bottom line. In the past, you'd be right. They'd have razed this place and been done with it, but the man wants to work with the neighborhoods where they set up. He wants to start building trust and community spirit instead of just dismantling the places they need and setting up new ones."

"Like Edward in *Pretty Woman*?" I scoffed. "That's Hollywood, not Corporate America. You've been sold a truckload of cow patties. The rich don't do anything that won't make them—and only them—richer."

"This guy's not like that. Apparently, Cole Rayburn was raised in rural Pennsylvania and spent most of his life as a working stiff, never involved with his grandfather's company. He even went by another name, although I don't know what it was. The lawyer said the only way he agreed to take over as CEO was if he got to do things his way."

I cocked my head. Growing up and using an assumed name would explain why his social footprint was lacking.

"The man firmly believes that it's time for the corporations to look beyond their bottom lines and do what's right for this country. As far as he's concerned, considering the way the last few years have been, fun and entertainment are the best ways to bring people together these days. He plans to turn this place into an upscale entertainment venue accessible to all. They'll have a dozen places open by Christmas, planning to bring in class acts to supplement Open Mic nights. They're looking to appeal to the working population as well as a wealthier clientele. It'll be a win-win situation for you all, you'll see."

I huffed out a breath, fighting to keep my anger and frustration under control.

"Listen to yourself. Wealthier clientele? As if the rich don't have enough places to play in LA. Do you honestly think they'll be happy to see the regulars we have here? The one's who've put money into your pockets all these years? Don't they deserve a playground, too?"

He straightened his spine. "Since when have you been so anti-money?"

I sighed. "I'm not anti-money, Jack. I need it to survive; so do all the others who work here. I'm anti-the-love-of-money and the way it changes people—rarely for the better. There's no way guys like Frank, Pete, and the rest of the regulars will feel at home here. The rich don't appreciate hobnobbing with the middle class."

"Now who's being a snob?"

"I'm not being a snob," I defended my attitude, reminded of Amalia's accusation the night of my birthday. What had she called me? A reverse snob? "I'm being a realist. I've worked a few country clubs and exclusive parties. This has disaster written all over it—not for you, and honestly I'm glad you're getting what you want, but for the rest of us. I sure as hell hope Mr. High and Mighty CEO has hired someone to manage the place who knows something about the bar business; otherwise, they'll lose their shirts, and as I said, the rich hate losing money."

I recalled Daddy ranting and raving about recessions and inflation, not to mention how much he'd paid in taxes.

"I'll admit it's a bold move that could easily bite them on the ass," Jack stated, rubbing the back of his neck. "But since that business is richer than Midas, they can probably use a few tax write-offs. They've promised not to close the club, just make it better. That's all I can hope for."

I shook my head. "Make it better, my aunt's patootie. That idea has catastrophe written all over it. Besides, opening more than one new place at a time is like fighting a war on two fronts. Eventually, you'll run out of soldiers. Ask Napolean or Hitler. Neither one did well."

He laughed. "I never thought of it that way. You know, every now and then you come out with something that has me wondering what kind of an education you really have. You're a damn fine bartender, and you can be funny as hell, but sometimes you surprise me, and that isn't easy to do."

Heat crept up my neck to my cheeks. If I didn't watch myself, my carefully crafted disguise would come apart in front of me.

"I'm just a good listener, and I read a lot," I argued. "So when is this happening?"

"June 30."

My eyes opened wider, and my jaw dropped.

"That's next week!"

He couldn't close the bar that soon. Where would I find another job?

He nodded. "It is. The lawyer tells me the new manager will be here by then and ready to start the renovations. I bought myself a first class ticket to Nome, leaving on July 1. No point in sitting around, watching things change. I'll be joining my son Joel and his family until I decide what I want to do with myself, but I want to be able to enjoy my grandkids while I still can. Eliza is four and Baby Jacob's almost two, and I haven't seen them since Luella's funeral. No one knows how much time they've got left, Andie. I'm not taking any more chances with mine. I'll be taking her ashes up there with me. She might've loved LA, but deep down, she missed those Midnight Suns and Northern Lights. We always meant to go back when we retired. Guess I'm just taking her home."

I blinked. How could I argue with that? This job had never been meant to be permanent, but lately I'd deluded myself into ignoring that. I'd also ignored the fact that my own father wasn't getting any younger. All he wanted was to see me safely settled before the time came, and if there was a grandson, so much the better.

I reached across the bar and touched Jack's hand.

"You do what you have to do. We all have to put ourselves first at some point." I had, and I didn't regret it for a second. "Rayburn Enterprises has been making money for decades. They aren't going to stop now. I'm sure they've done their homework, and the new manager will be the best money can buy … it's just that I'm going to miss you. Have you told the rest of the staff yet?"

"No. I'm going to do it at the end of the night. Since we're usually closed on Sunday, Monday, and Tuesday, it'll give them time to deal with the news." He smiled sadly. "You know, the hardest part of all this is leaving you behind. I don't know why you decided you wanted to work for me. We both know you can do better. You may hide behind that little Texas cowgirl façade, but you're educated—and don't give me that crap about your mixologist's degree. You've got real schooling behind you, but something happened to make you set it all aside. I won't pry. We all come to LA looking for something different, and we're allowed to keep our secrets. Now, I'm going to let you finish getting ready to open. I'll talk to you later. This is going to be a good move for everyone, Andie, mark my word."

I nodded, too choked up and embarrassed to speak. Why was it that when I thought everything was going well, Fate smacked me up the side of the head and reminded me that I only thought I was in charge?

* * *

When I'd left work that night, after Jack had informed the staff of the sale, the place had been like a funeral parlor with the people congregating in small groups, bemoaning the loss of what had been a big part of their lives. No one blamed Jack for selling, but damn, it had been a bitter pill to swallow. There had been tears, anger, and shock, but by the time we opened the next night, everyone had come to grips with it, making plans to find interim jobs or quit outright. Like me, many saw the corporate acquisition as the kiss of death. I still didn't know what I was going to do and that was a huge problem.

By midweek, word had gotten around that we'd been sold, so when the **Under New Management** signs went up earlier tonight, no one was surprised. Since the rumor mill worked faster than any bona fide news outlet in the world—other than the Yellow Press who made it up as they went along—everyone who'd ever spent any time here was bemoaning the loss of their home away from home. Thursday nights were usually quiet, but this weekend was our last one before the renovations started. I might want to rant, rave, and throw a good old-fashioned temper tantrum at having my plans fall apart, but deep down I'd always known things couldn't last. Pasting a smile on my face, I rang the cowbell and set down the tray of drinks for the server to pick up.

"Order up, Jess!" I bellowed across the bar into the noisy room to be heard over the DJ's current musical offering, something by Pink.

I reached for the next chit on the order wheel, but before I got to work on it, I looked over my shoulder, making sure that all of my bar patrons had what they needed, including Jack and the Rayburn lawyer. Satisfied that they did, I returned to the task at hand.

Jack had signed the contracts earlier. He and the lawyer had done it at the bar in front of the staff and we'd all celebrated with a glass of champagne, surprisingly the good stuff. The last time I'd had any had been on my birthday.

"Order up, Luce," I yelled, this time trying to be heard over The Weeknd, setting down the tray, and ringing the cowbell.

I checked the bar. Jack was gone, but the lawyer was still there. The man had reminded me of Dan, all very prim and proper while he'd been working, but once he'd put the contract inside his briefcase, that front had slipped. Instead of more champagne or beer, he'd jumped into the hard stuff, top shelf scotch, doubles, neat.

I walked down the bar toward him.

"Hey, cupcake, how about another scotch? Your boss called it a night, but we can still party."

My heart had stopped at the nickname, resuming its beating slowly once I recalled that it was only a nickname.

"Sure thing, suhh." I climbed up the ladder and took down the most expensive scotch in the bar.

"You can leave it down. I'll want more. What good is an expense account if you don't use it?"

I nodded, poured him another generous double … no ice, and added it to his tab.

"So, you're Andie Harper. Jack certainly thinks a lot of you. He had me rewrite the paragraph concerning the staff vacation pay and benefits three times before he was satisfied with it. I thought our offer was generous enough, but he threatened to back out of the deal if that clause wasn't to his satisfaction. You must be damn good at everything you do to have a man willing to throw it all away for a roll in the hay with you. Maybe if I got some of what you've got to give, I would, too."

Filthy mouthed jerk!

I fisted my hands at my side, sensing myself moving toward hurricane mode once more. This was not the time for a hissy fit. If I ruined this for Jack and the staff … I turned away, busying myself at the bar, checking supplies that needed no checking.

"Good girl. You know when to keep your mouth shut, too. Not sure how Mr. Rayburn's going to feel about that new clause, but he did tell me to make the deal no matter what, and believe me, honey, you have a sweet deal. My new boss is harder to read than *War and Peace*."

He laughed, the sound of it telling me he should quit drinking now before he said something he might regret. Should I tell him he was on camera? Would he care? Maybe he would if he realized it recorded sound as well as picture. Luella had made the upgrade after they'd helped catch a rapist picking up girls in bars, putting scopolamine in their drinks, and then offering to take them home. The equipment had worked so well, they'd decided to keep it. Everything he'd just said was already uploaded to the server for posterity.

Like every other blowhard I'd met here, usually the guys with the six-figure salaries, the more he drank, the more he liked the sound of his own voice.

"I used to know exactly where I sat, the way things were going to play out when we bought a crappy business like this place, but Cole … do you know I've never even met the man face-to-face, and I'm his God damn corporate lawyer. The press have dubbed him a modern-day Howard Hughes. After his parents were killed, he vanished into the Alleghenies and was raised by his maternal grandparents on a frigging farm. What the hell does he know about business?"

"I'm sure I don't know," I answered, desperate to get away. What did he think I was? Clairvoyant?

It was a mystery to me how someone could hide in the shadows and run such a large corporation, especially since my dang picture was on the front page of one tabloid or another almost as often as the President's was.

God answers prayers in the most mysterious ways.

A woman screeched, a sound I recognized as Luce's voice. I stood on the stool. From my perch, I could see two guys had shoved one another, and in the process, they'd knocked her down, spilling the tray of drinks all over her. Tank was already there, one guy in each hand, but Luce needed help.

"Sorry, I've gotta go."

I hurried around the side of the bar, sending Jess in to mind the store, while I helped Luce clean up. Ten minutes later, she was back at work in the dry clothes she kept in her locker. Reluctantly, I returned to the bar, pleased to see Slimy Stuckey, as I'd nicknamed the lawyer since he reminded me of the one in Pretty Woman, was gone.

Goodbye and good riddance.

Jess came over to me. "The lawyer's gone. Piece of shite has a mouth like a sewer and the manners of a pig. He got a call and lit out of here as if his shorts were on fire. He didn't even pay his tab."

I shrugged. "He's on the company payroll. I'll set it aside for the new manager. Now, I have a feeling tonight's going to be a long one."

"Yeah, one fight usually leads to another. The place is buzzing. I just hoped the acts are good enough to break through the melancholy and have everyone laughing and not catcalling. Where's Jack?"

"He left but he gave me the line-up before he did. We'll be fine."

Two hours later, we were not fine. We were anything but fine. Maybe it was a prophetic sign of what was to come, but the acts so far had been brutal, the worst I'd ever seen since working here, and the crowd, needing laughter to unwind, had ended up more worked up than when they'd come in and hadn't kept their displeasure quiet.

Sometimes the crowds could be cruel. But The Pickleback was better than some places where the performers worked behind chicken wire to keep from being pelted with bottles and trash. Jack had never allowed that, and tossing anything at the stage brought Tank to the table and an end to the evening.

By midnight, Slimy Stucky wasn't the only drunk at the bar. I'd had to cut off three of my regulars and was still in the process of getting that settled when two women got into a hair-pulling contest over some mediocre stud, a biker who might've been worth fighting over when *Easy Rider* was playing in the theaters. They might as well have been two bitches in heat fighting over a well-hung dog. Tank was still dealing with the guys I'd cut off, so seeing no option, I stepped on the stool and went across the bar landing between them. With an arm around each of them, I stood there.

"Jess, grab those purses and cell phones. These ladies are leaving."

"You bitch, what gives you the right to lay a finger on me? I'll sue you and this bar."

"Go ahead, sugar. See that shiny clock up there? Smile, you're on camera."

"You have no right to film me without my consent," one of them slurred, struggling to get out of my grip.

"And you have no expectation of privacy in a public place." I reached the door with my charges. "Here Tank. These lovely ladies have had enough fun for the night. Kindly escort them out and see they don't get back in again. Here are their purses and their phones."

"How the hell do I know you didn't rob me blind, bitch?" one of the women accused Jess.

I smiled. "Aren't you precious? Cameras, sugar. Remember."

Tank laughed. "This way, ladies. I'll get you a cab." He looked at me. "What about the tab?"

I shrugged. "Only one drink. It's on the house now. They can consider it a going away present. By the way, ladies, it's a permanent band from here. Don't plan on coming back."

I returned to the bar, grabbed twenty bucks from my tip jar, and rang up the sale. That was definitely money well spent.

"Jess, cover for me? It's time for me to introduce the last act."

She came over to the bar.

"I'll have to sneak into jack's office and watch the replay of that. You crossed the top of the bar like an avenging angel, then wrestled those two hellcats to the ground as if they were twin steers in a rodeo competition. I knew you told me you'd competed but … Quite the feat given your size."

I wiped my hands on the bar towel and shrugged.

"Y'all know what they say, the bigger they are, the harder they fall. Besides, I didn't have time to think about it with those two bitches in heat on one another like flies on a cow patty, hissing, screaming, biting, and ripping out hanks of hair. I wasn't in the mood for a cat fight, although I'm sure some of the others were getting ready to place bets on them." I shook my head. "The new owner won't tolerate stuff like that. He wants to raise the wallet level in here, make the place more sophisticated, and attract better talent as well as smarter critics.

Those two might've done well mudwrestling, but that's about it. The man may be aiming too high, but the place can use a facelift."

"I'm not sure a facelift will do the trick," Jess laughed.

She didn't know the truth. A little cosmetic surgery worked magic.

Thankfully, the rest of the evening went smoothly, since I was running on empty. Hopefully, the same would be true for tomorrow. As soon as everyone cashed out, I opened the safe and put away the night's receipts before calling for my UBER.

CHAPTER EIGHT

"Dang it!"

I grabbed a napkin and wrapped it around my knuckle, dropping the paring knife I was using to slice lemons and limes. The acid in the fruit made the small cut burn like a son of a gun. Seriously, after last night, how much worse could things get?

I unwrapped my finger, removed the damaged latex glove, pleased to see the cut was barely bleeding. Going to the small First-Aid kit I kept under the counter, I grabbed a band-aid and covered it before slipping on clean latex gloves to finish cutting the fruit I needed for cocktails.

I sighed. This Friday night was shaping up to be the busiest one yet. Since I overslept my alarm, the day had disaster written on it from the moment I'd opened my eyes. It had been as if I'd started one of those domino chains and everything had gone downhill after that.

I'd been ten minutes late arriving and hadn't stopped since I'd taken over the bar from Jack. The burger sent up from the kitchen an hour ago had a bite out of it, but cold, congealed beef wasn't a particular favorite of mine. I tossed it into the trash and hurried to fill another order of Picklebacks. As tonight's featured drinks, they were moving well.

By eight, I'd dropped two glasses, narrowly averted spilling juice on myself, and wasn't in the best of moods, although I did my best to hide it from the customers. I was worried not only about the future of my plans to find Mr. Right, but also about what I would tell Amalia on Sunday. The way I saw it, with this job gone, I was out of options. I had no choice but to go home defeated and accept whatever Fate and Daddy had in store for me.

"Dallas, get me two jugs of today's special while I go powder my nose."

I snapped my head up. While I had nothing against the city I claimed as my birthplace, I hated being called by its name. Was Andie really that much harder to say and remember? Glenda wasn't the sharpest tool in the shed, but surely if she could remember six letters, she could recall five?

The redhead with more boobs than brains stood there doing the peepee dance. What was this? Her third break? She'd only started two hours ago. Someone needed to explain the correlation between water in and urine out—either that or get her some adult diapers.

I swallowed my irritation and pasted a smile on my face. Servers were supposed to pour their own draft beer while I dealt with the mixed drinks and fancier cocktails.

"Bless your heart, I'll be happy to. I'm not doing anything else right now."

"Thanks, I knew I could count on you."

She grinned, oblivious to my sarcasm as I finished making a Bloody Mary and set it on the tray next to the two Margaritas, the Manhattan, and the Singapore Sling another waitress had ordered. I rang the cowbell once more.

"Boys behaving tonight?" I asked as she put up her chit for the mixed drinks she needed, too.

"They're watching themselves. No one wants to get thrown out when the drinks are free. They all heard about last night's evictions."

One of the regulars had just signed a contract to be the opening act for a comic taking the country by storm. It was a big deal, especially when none of us had recognized the talent scout in the audience the night he'd gotten his big break. Raffey had been up on that stage every Friday night since before I'd started here, and the man was a comedic genius. He deserved this break. While his friends might envy the hell out of him, they were all eager to celebrate the accomplishment—and imbibe in the free drinks that went with it. Another Pickleback tradition gone.

I chuckled. "Can't beat that with a stick."

She rolled her eyes. "Is that another of your sayings?"

"Sure'nuff is. It means you won't get a better deal. Now git and do your business. Time's a wasting."

"You really should remember that you're in LA now, not some Podunk town where they roll up the sidewalks at night. The new management wants to make this a classier place; I don't think your folksy expressions are going to fit in. You should consider a speech coach or something—that is if you want to keep your job."

While I might like to dump the container of Bloody Mary mix I was holding over her head, I smiled more broadly instead.

"Thanks for the advice. I'll do my best to remember that."

I bit my tongue to stop myself from saying something cutting that I might regret.

She nodded, turned, and rushed away from the bar.

I did my best to get along with all of the staff, but Glenda would try the patience of a saint. It was no secret that, like Jess, she was hoping this job led to something better.

"One of these days, you're going to have to sit down and teach me how to insult people the way you do with a 'butter won't melt in my mouth' look. You were fantastic with those two witches last night, and just now … I don't know how you do it."

I turned to glance at Jess and grinned, batting my eyelids as if they were hummingbirds.

"Little old me? Do tell."

She burst out laughing.

"She's not the only one who's going to need to go if you keep making faces like that."

"Faces like what?"

I cocked my head and batted my eyelids once more.

"You should've signed up for your own twenty-minute gig months ago. You might've been the one celebrating that big break tonight. You're hilarious."

She moved to the draft taps and started filling her order.

I shook my head. "No, thanks. You might want to be in the limelight, but I'd rather cower here behind the bar in the dark where no one can see me." At least for the little time left to me. I would be the center of attraction soon enough.

She rolled her eyes. "As if. There isn't a person in here who can ignore you, and you know it. The second you step on stage—"

I shook my head. "Don't remind me. I didn't sign on to do those sixty second intros, but I'd just started, and Jack broke his ankle. Since he couldn't get up on stage, he decided I could do it. Don't know where he got that idea ... Thankfully, all I have to do is read the intros he or the acts give me ... which reminds me, have you seen him? The first comedian is due up in twenty minutes or so, and he hasn't given me tonight's script."

"He's probably in his office, but I'll stop by and tell him you need him. I've got a reading for a part in a sitcom. Maybe I should try it with a Texas drawl."

Jess and I had grown close since I'd started here. She'd helped me deal with more than one loser and had commiserated with me when the guy I'd really liked, the one I thought might be the one, had turned out to be Mr. Married With Two Kids, a Mortgage, and a Pregnant Wife.

While I wanted to keep a low profile, she had different priorities, hoping to be discovered and become Hollywood's next sought-after leading lady. She was cute and quite talented, certainly a head and shoulders above Glenda, but she lacked that quality that would make her attract the attention she needed. I intended to fix that, but it needed to wait until my charade was over.

I leaned across the bar and touched her hand.

"Accents and expressions don't mean a dang thing. Our words don't define us, our actions do."

She laughed so hard that she snorted, drawing the attention of the closest patrons.

"Then, after last night, I'd say you were one hell of a bad ass. Who knew?"

I wiped my hands on the bar towel and shrugged. "All in a day's work."

Jess harrumphed. "Well, the new manager can change whatever the hell he wants as long as I still have a job. A flashier crowd and higher prices should mean better tips. I'm getting more callbacks, but until I get a part, that doesn't put food on the table. I've gotten used to eating three square meals a day."

I grinned "Don't you give me that. You ain't dirt poor yet, and ya'll know it. I happen to know you're working on that beer commercial while you're on this paid vacation, and I'm sure something else will come along. You're too talented to ignore. Now, before those guys at table nine start hollering, best you deliver those drinks."

"Yes, ma'am," she mocked in an exaggerated Texan accent before winking at me and walking away.

Luce collected her tray of cocktails, and I moved over to the beer tap and started pouring Glenda's first pitcher. Looking up, I noticed that someone had taken the last empty seat at the bar. Had he been there long? I usually knew every time a seat was vacated or filled, but tonight, as busy as the place was, it was easy to overlook a change.

I finished filling the first jug and started the second. Once it was done, I set the two jugs in the pickup area for Glenda to grab when she got back. She could wait a few minutes for her cocktails. Snatching up some coasters, I headed down the bar until I reached the last seat.

The man had his back to me, examining the crowd, but I knew without seeing his face that he was new here. I would never forget broad shoulders like those. Perhaps he'd come to support a friend making his debut tonight. We did have two new acts rounding out the regulars, both of whom were crowd favorites.

I leaned across the bar to be heard over the music. A familiar scent tickled my nose.

"Howdy, stranger, what can I git ya?"

I slapped the coaster down. He was welcome to support his friend all he wanted, but he needed to drink if he wanted a seat at my bar.

He turned around, his eyes growing wide, his chocolate gaze raking me up and down, sending electric shocks through me. The man was clean shaven, with short blond hair, and skin tanned by the sun. He had a straight nose, full lips, and eyelashes that some women would fight to the death over—me included. Under a leather jacket, he wore a plain black t-shirt that set off his well-toned but not overblown muscles, pecs, and abs. Judging by the height of him above the bar, he was more than six-feet tall. No doubt his legs would be encased in tight denim that would fit in all the right places. There was something familiar about him, something that stimulated my memory, but to no avail.

I would've had to be blind not to notice the smoldering in his eyes when his gaze finished his perusal of me and connected with mine. Just like that, I was a steaming volcano filled with lava and ready to erupt. My cheeks burned, and if he kept looking at me like that, I might just melt.

His grin broadened and like a bolt of lightning out of the blue, I realized why he looked familiar. The man across from me was none other than Handsome Harry. Sure, he no longer had a beard, and his hair was cut short, but the eyes were the same. Joy filled me, quickly replaced by panic. I wanted to run, but where could I go?

It was over. This was it. The moment I'd feared. My identity was about to be revealed and months and months of hard work would be undone. I hadn't found Mr. Right yet, and once my secret was out, everyone would know who I was, and I never would. On the one hand, I wanted to scream in frustration; on the other, I had wanted to see him again, if only to apologize for Becki's rudeness.

I grabbed the bar counter and waited for him to drop his bomb.

He smiled. "You're a cut above the last bartender who served me. Let me try one of your signature drinks."

Surprised, I nodded. "One Pickleback coming right up."

I turned away, confused and unexpectedly hopeful. Was it possible that, thanks to the cosmetic surgery, he didn't recognize me? That was what I wanted, right? To be a new woman, completely different from the troll I'd been, and yet, the fact that he didn't know me hurt.

"Wait."

I looked over my shoulder, expecting him to identify me now.

"Is the kitchen still open? I flew in from New York this afternoon and haven't had time for dinner."

As nervous as I suddenly was, I forced myself to stay calm and not answer with a bad joke.

His accent wasn't one that I would associate with New York, but these days people moved around a lot more than they used to do. I hadn't been able to pinpoint it on my birthday either.

Not wanting him to see how unsettled I was, I nodded.

"The kitchen does pub grub for another hour. Would ya'll like to see a menu?"

"That would be fine."

Smiling, I turned away from him, hoping my pulse and breathing would settle. I quickly made his drink and grabbed a menu. If he didn't recognize me, the possibilities were endless, but I needed to be careful and not say anything that could have him wondering if we'd met before.

After placing his two-glass drink on coasters in front of him, I handed him the menu and went back to work, forcing myself to shove the potential disaster to the back of my head and fill Glenda's cocktail order before she came after me to do it.

Jess signaled me, and I hurried to the end of the bar where she waited.

I looked around. "Where's Jack?"

"On the phone with Rayburn's lawyer. Something's come up that has to be dealt with right away. He says you'll have to wing it for the first act. Here are the names and the order in which they'll perform. Good luck."

"Wing it? With the place as busy as it is tonight?"

With Handsome Harry in the audience? Was Jack crazy? I wasn't a comedian. I was the bartender. Sure, I threw in a gag of my own now and then, but...

"You'll be fine. You're a natural. Trust me. Just tell them about your morning, and they'll be rolling on the floor. Your job is to warm up the crowd and get them ready to laugh, both things you do incredibly well."

She hurried away to check on her tables.

I rolled my eyes. Could anything else go wrong tonight?

I looked at the list and exhaled the breath that I hadn't realized I was holding. The first name was Josh Ames, a high school drama teacher by day and a would-be comedian each weekend. He wasn't looking to move on from that, content with his life. He was a crowd favorite, so that wouldn't be too hard. Hopefully, Jack would be off the phone with

Slimy Stucky soon, and I could get the necessary material before the first of the new acts went on.

I shoved the list into my back pocket. Knowing there was no way out, I hurried down the bar to Handsome Harry again, noticing that he'd finished his drink.

"Like it?" I asked automatically, something I did each time someone ordered a Pickleback for the first time.

"It's not bad, but I wouldn't want to drink too many of them."

"Yeah, the pickle juice is really high in sodium." I watched him for any signs that he recognized me, both pleased and disappointed when I couldn't see any. "Have you decided what you'll have?"

"A pound of wings, suicide sauce on the side, fries, and coleslaw."

I punched it into my tablet and pressed send. The kitchen would get it right away.

"And to drink?"

"How about a large draft? It's hot in here." He removed his jacket, revealing his tanned arms.

His words didn't reflect the heat and interest in his eyes, and I was sure there was more to his comment about the heat than a leather jacket … he had another kind of hotness on his mind, and I could appreciate that. I might've recognized him, but if he hadn't figured out who I was, then it was all good. Lust was as good a place as any to start. I could work with this. Yes, I could indeed.

Swallowing my pent up desires, I nodded.

"Coming right up."

After pouring his draft and delivering it, I got ready to go up on stage.

"Luce," I called to the waitress who took my place behind the bar while I was introducing the acts. I wasn't going to give Glenda that job. "I've got an intro. Mind the bar, for me?"

"Sure thing, Andie." She moved closer to me. "I wonder if the new owner will let you keep introducing the acts. You should use your own material. That story you told us in the breakroom when we came in had me laughing so hard, I almost had an accident. You have a natural talent for comedy."

I chuckled. "Well, believe me, it wasn't that hilarious when it happened. By the way, lucky number twelve has a plate of wings and things coming up from the kitchen."

"Got it.

I left the bar and worked my way through the crowd to the stage. Raffey, well on his way to total alcoholic oblivion, reached for me none too steadily. I grabbed his arm to keep him from faceplanting onto the floor.

"Whoa there, buddy. You might have a gallon too many in your tank."

He smiled at me, that dopey, sappy smile drunks get just before they're either going to pass out or hurl all over you.

"Marry me, Andie. I'm serious this time," he slurred, his breath strong enough to knock over a horse.

"You're serious every time you ask." I chuckled. "As flattered as I am to have a man like y'all make me that offer, I'm not the marryin' type. Like the song says, 'Papa was a Rollin' Stone,' and I'm a chip off the old boulder."

I led Raffey back to his seat.

"Now, sugar, I've got to get up on stage and introduce Josh. You sit here and listen."

He stumbled back into his chair and nodded.

I knew his feelings weren't hurt. He proposed every time he got drunk, but the man and I had never even been on a date together. Rumor had it he'd once been a priest. I didn't know what he'd done to get defrocked … that was between him and the Almighty … but I had no intention of contributing to his delinquency. No, as of tonight, I had a different partner in mind for that.

Turning away, I headed up to the stage to introduce the first act. I couldn't see the bar from the stage, so there was no chance of focusing my attention on Handsome Harry, but even though I couldn't see him, I felt him.

The DJ stopped the music, and I stepped up to the mic. The room quieted for a moment and then filled with sound again.

"Quiet down, fellas." I waited a few seconds and then continued. "Howdy, folks. It's mighty fine to have you all come out for our second last night at The Pickleback. I'm looking forward to seeing you back with us come Labor Day once we're all gussied up like a fine lady going out to dinner. Tonight, we've got some of your old favorites back to entertain you and a couple of new acts to tickle your fancies. Our first act one of my favorites."

I licked my lips.

Here goes nothing.

I grinned. "Ya'll know that I find LA to be a puzzling town and many of the things I've seen and bought here continue to mystify me. I was plum tuckered when I got home last night and overslept. Fighting cougars and coyotes is hard work." People laughed, no doubt those who'd heard about my exploits. "Any of you fine folks invest money in them room-darkening curtains? Normally, I leave mine open just a smidgeon in case I have to answer nature's call, but last night I pulled those shades tighter than a noose. When I awoke, my watch told me it was after two, but it was still as dark as midnight in my room. I dragged my sorry butt into the kitchen and saw that it was bright and sunny out. I put on the coffee and put my frozen waffles in the toaster and then headed back to take my shower. Suddenly, the fire alarm started blaring to beat the band, and someone pounded on my door. There I was as naked as the day I was born, shampoo in my hair and in my eyes, the alarm shrieking, and my landlady screaming that she'd called the fire department. I didn't bother rinsing off, just shut off the tap, gave myself a lick and a promise toweling, rushed back into my sleeping cave, grabbed the pair of drawers from the shelf where I kept them, and … Ladies, if you've ever tried to pull up a wet bathing suit, y'all know that's not an easy thing to do. Well, my eyes are stinging, there's enough noise to wake the dead, and when them drawers are almost up, they refuse to move an inch higher. I'm hopping around like a cowpoke who stepped into the branding fire, and the alarm is still singing away, the landlady's a calling my name, and I'm stuck in my knickers. Confused, I whipped open the curtain, removed the underwear and saw the problem. I was trying to put one of the leg holes around my waist. Don't ask me how it happened, I haven't the foggiest idea. Let me just say them dang string underwear never fail to confuse me."

Laughter filled the room. I smiled. Intro number one done.

"Needless to say, I managed to get dressed, rescued the waffles, and the coffee before the firemen arrived. They insisted on looking around and leaving me a number in case I ever needed help again. All in all, that was the most excitement I've had in a week of Sundays. And now, keep those chuckles and guffaws going for our very own, Josh Ames."

I handed the mic to Josh.

216

He grinned. "Let's hear it for Andie. She's without a doubt the best and funniest bartender in all of LA."

The crowd applauded. I gave a bad impression of a curtsey and returned to the bar.

Luce set down the draft she'd poured for one of the guys.

"I added it to his tab." She indicated the mug. "That was just as funny the second time as it was the first. You need one more for number ten. He claims he's running a tab."

"Thanks, and he is." I looked over and saw that Handsome Harry's meal had been served. "I'll see you in forty-five minutes."

Luce nodded and went back to her tables. I poured the draft, delivered it, and checked on the rest of my customers, before moving to the end of the bar.

I set a few more napkins down next to the platter and indicated the wings.

"Are they hot enough for you?"

Suicide sauce could burn the roof off my mouth in seconds.

"They're good and hot—just the way I like them." His smirk implied he liked other things hot as well. "You were pretty good, too. Andie, is it?"

As a rule, I kept the flirting light, but this was Handsome Harry, a man I'd been attracted to from the moment I'd seen him, a man who'd massaged my feet.

"Yeah, that's me. I don't normally deliver my own material, but the boss is kind of busy right now. The comics usually write their own opening laughs to put the crowd in the right mood."

"Makes sense. I'm LJ by the way."

"First and last?" I quipped, wondering what the letters represented.

"First and middle. It'll take some time for every man in the place, me included, to get that image of you, as the Good Lord made you, out of his mind."

"I hadn't thought of that. I hope it won't keep you up all night."

I batted my eyelids a time or two before meeting his gaze. I'd never been this brazen before.

Staring into his cocoa eyes, I forced down the heat crawling up from my toes to my nose, not thrilled to have it settle in my middle, causing my crotch to dampen. I reached for the empty beer glass. Luce had given him a glass of water, too.

"Going to be in LA long?" I was curious to know if seeing him again was an option.

He laughed. "That depends. How did you know I didn't live here?"

I shrugged. "You just said you flew in from New York and hadn't eaten."

He held up a half-eaten wing. "Good to know that you pay attention."

"Always."

I was getting hotter by the minute, and there was nothing I could take off to cool down.

"Then, we'll probably see more of each other since I'll be spending time here."

Seeing more of him certainly appealed.

"Can I get you anything else before I get back to work?"

"Water's good for now, thanks."

"I'll check on ya later."

And with that, I sashayed to the other end of the bar, making sure I twitched my butt a little more than usual. When I glanced to see if he was watching me, bitter disappointment filled me. He was stuffing his face as if he hadn't eaten in ages. So much for my imagining that he was as hungry for me as he was for those wings.

After that, everything got so crazy busy that I barely had time to think. Jack had taken off as soon as he'd gotten off the phone with the lawyer, leaving me to clean up and cash out again tonight.

By the time I stepped off the stage after the last intro, I was dog-tired. Between making drinks for the waitresses and serving my own customers, the only conversation I'd had with LJ—I liked Handsome Harry better—had involved clearing away his dirty dishes and refilling his beer, not that the man was a heavy drinker.

The last act, a new one, was nothing special, and people had been drifting out for a while. By the time the DJ finished there were only a few diehards left. I went to collect the glassware from the area the comedians used and then returned to the bar. While I'd been gone, LJ had left.

Had he paid one of the other girls? Picking up the tab two nights in a row would really cut into my income. Dang it! I'd intended to give him my new cell number, something I never did, but I had really hoped to see him again—although that might be dangerous if he did realize who I was.

All along, I'd planned to pretend to be someone I wasn't, but it suddenly dawned on me that in this case, since I knew who he was, if he found out who I was before I was ready for the big reveal, he might be angry. If the show were on the other foot, I would be. Dang it. Why was nothing ever easy? It was probably just as well that he'd left.

CHAPTER NINE

Going down to the end of the bar, I picked up the beer glass and smiled. Handsome Harry had left a card, one of the bar ones in the holder on the counter, and some money. I flipped the card over. It read, *See you soon, Andie,* and was signed, *LJ.* Unfortunately, nothing on the card would help that happen. I opened the bills and stared at the image of Ulysses S. Grant.

"Hello, Mr. President."

The man had not only covered his tab, but he'd also left me a hefty tip.

"Come back anytime, LJ, any time at all," I mumbled before clearing off the rest of the bar and ringing up the sale.

As usual, Glenda was the first to cash out, and Luce and Jess were doing so now. By the time I'd reconciled my cash and put the bag in the safe with the others, the bar was empty. With the lights turned up, the place looked more tired and tacky than ever. Jack was right. It was time to walk away from it. Here and there, some of the decorative items were missing, no doubt claimed by the crowd who wanted a piece of the place. Jack wouldn't care, and I doubted Cole Rayburn would either. It was almost two when I used my cell phone to call my UBER.

Tank, always the last one to leave and lock up, waited with me by the door until the car arrived.

"It's raining out there, Andie."

I shook my head. Of course it was. "See you tomorrow night, Tank."

"See you, Andie."

I rushed out into the warm California rain, opened the door and hopped into the back of the vehicle the way I had every night since I'd started working at The Pickleback.

"G'Morning, Phil. How was business tonight?"

"Steady. What about you? I picked up a few fares here earlier."

"Busy, yeah, but without last night's drama. The crowd was a mite more civilized."

"Given the way you described that fight you broke up last night that wouldn't be hard. I'm just glad that you're my last call. Looking forward to getting into my air-conditioned house and crawling between the sheets with my wife. You would think the rain would eliminate the humidity. Instead, it's just made it worse."

"I know what you mean. The heat back home is bone dry, and while the temperature can go over a hundred and ten, it's not as oppressive as this. Investing in that window air conditioner was a blessing. I still owe you for letting me know your brother-in-law had it for sale."

"No biggie. Now, I've been listening to people complaining all night that the bar's been sold to some outfit from the east coast that's going to turn it into a place for the rich and famous. Is it true? Did Jack sell out to some fancy corporation, hanging the staff and the regulars out to dry? That just doesn't sound like him."

I sighed. If real news got around as fast as gossip, a whole slew of reporters would be out of work in no time.

"He didn't hang anyone out to dry. We'll be fine, and the bar will only be closed for the summer, but he did what he needed to do for him. Since Luella's death, he tried, but his heart just wasn't in it," I defended my former boss. "He's moving to Alaska to be near his son. The official announcement will be in Monday's paper. The company building the hotel next door bought him out which shouldn't surprise anyone. It's a tried and true method used to eliminate the competition. Come Labor Day, the crowd may well be a different one, but everyone will be welcome. Most of the staff will be back, and the place will still have live entertainment, but it won't necessarily only be comedians. There's going to be Open Mic during the week and some of the regulars are bound to come back."

Phil whistled. "I heard them say the place will be closed a few weeks. That's going to put a hell of a hole in your income."

"Yeah, but we've all been given vacation pay to tide us over. Plus, I've got enough saved to keep me going. I'm planning to enjoy my time off for now. Then, when the bar reopens under its new name—and don't ask me what that's going to be— I'll decide whether or not I'll stay."

If I did stay, it would only be for a few weeks at best.

"Any bar would be happy to have you. If you decide to move let me know, and I'll ask around."

"Thanks. I'd appreciate that."

He pulled up to the curb, and I handed him my usual fifteen bucks.

"See you tomorrow night."

"Stay safe."

"I will."

Getting out of the Suburban, I rushed through the rain and up the stairs to my second-floor apartment. I unlocked the door and let myself in, closing the door behind me and locking all four locks. A girl living alone in LA could never be too careful.

After making sure the locks were all secured, I dropped my purse onto the small table near the door, and placed my keys in the basket. The apartment, actually smaller in size than my bedroom at the ranch, consisted of four rooms—a living room separated from the kitchen by a breakfast bar, a bathroom, and a bedroom. The place had come furnished. Everything was clean, but all from the seventies with the color scheme to match—dark brown sofa and chair over an orange rug. I'd never actually seen a shag rug before, but I loved it. The only items that were mine were the flatscreen TV, the air conditioner I'd bought from Phil's brother-in-law, the single brew coffeemaker, and the painting I'd made of the sunset.

I walked over to the easy chair, sitting to remove the boots and the socks I'd worn all day. I massaged the soles of my feet in the carpet, sighing in ecstasy. If the perfect man for me existed; he was the one who'd rubbed my sore feet months ago, the one I'd found sitting across the bar from me tonight—the one who hadn't recognized me, making all of my fantasies possible.

Unlike the killer heels I'd worn on my birthday, the custom-made cowboy boots had two-inch heels and a built-in lift that gave me another inch behind the bar. The soft leather boots were molded to my feet and quite comfortable, but after standing for almost ten hours, my feet and my back ached.

I wriggled my bare toes before trotting across the cool tile floor and walking down the hallway to my bedroom. Unlike the sofa and chair, the queen bed was a new one, although the pine combination dresser and closet must have spent time in someone's cottage years ago. The bed was covered in a beige quilt, and as I'd said on stage, I'd recently replaced the thin matching drapes with brown room-darkening ones that did indeed turn the room into a cave. Since I worked by night and slept by day, it was necessary.

I removed my tie and suspenders, placing them across the back of the chair. I took off my pants and white blouse, tossing them in the laundry basket with my underwear, and reached for the oversized Lakers jersey and sleep shorts I wore to bed. They were actually more comfortable than the cotton nighties I'd worn for years.

Going into the small bathroom, I flipped the light switch, bathing the room in LED light. Each time I looked in the mirror, I did a doubletake, still not convinced that the beautiful woman looking back at me wasn't the ugly duckling I'd once been. There was no sign of the surgery I'd had. Nothing to point to those droopy eyelids, lard nose, and weak chin—and as for my breasts, they were firm and perky, even under the oversized shirt.

Using the products provided by Shangri-la, I cleaned and moisturized my face before brushing my hair and my teeth. Once my toilette was complete, I headed to bed, knowing my dreams would be full of Handsome Harry tonight.

* * *

The following morning, I was up at eleven with the alarm. The skies were still overcast, the humidity oppressive, but there was no rain in the forecast. That was just as well since I seemed to be under a dark, dreary cloud of my own this morning. If I'd dreamed of Handsome Harry, I didn't remember it, but I did know that unless he showed up again tonight, I had no way to find him.

I showered in the two-square-foot shower, wishing once again that the bathroom had a tub. How long had it been since I'd indulged in a hot, relaxing, bubble bath?

Finished, I dried off, used the blow dryer on my hair the way I'd been taught, and turned the ends under with the electric hairbrush, shoving one side behind my ear. I smoothed on the day lotion I used for my face. It contained sunscreen. I never left home without it. Since tonight might be my last night at The Pickleback, I added eyeshadow, mascara, and a touch of blush to my daily cosmetic routine.

Going into the tiny kitchen, I managed to make myself coffee and toasts without setting off the fire alarm. I settled in front of the TV and turned to the news channel to catch up on what was happening in the world. I might not like the state of the union and what was going on in the elsewhere, but I needed to know. As usual, the wars overseas dominated the headlines, together with reports of more vicious weather. The newest hurricane brewing in the Caribbean showed signs of rapid escalation. It was all bad. Beryl had left a track of destruction throughout the islands, Texas, reaching up as far as parts of Canada. Sadly, there didn't seem to be much anyone could do but cross their fingers and pray.

By three, I was dressed in a clean white blouse and black pants, my suspenders and tie in my purse when I walked into The Pickleback, expecting to find Jack behind the bar. He wasn't.

"Where's Jack?"

Eugene was one of the part-timers who sometimes covered for him.

"Don't know. He called me in this morning. Said he had business to attend to and asked me to come in for the afternoon and stick around in case you needed help tonight." The man shook his head. "This place is full of memories for him, good and bad. It's probably damn hard for him to leave it, but he did leave an envelope back here for you."

"Sure'nuff. Goodbyes are always bittersweet. I'll be up to relieve you after I get a bite to eat— didn't manage to get any grub in me last night. I would be mighty grateful if you did stick around for a while." I looked around the room that was remarkably busy for a Saturday afternoon. "If it continues like this, I'm sure I can use your help tonight."

He nodded. "No problem, Andie. Always happy to help out."

I hoped Jack would swing by tonight. I didn't feel as if I'd had a chance to say a proper goodbye and thank you. It wasn't his fault that my plans had fizzled. They probably hadn't been realistic from the onset. Amalia and the twins would've recognized that, but they'd gotten me my chance and I loved them for it.

I hurried to the kitchen, ordered a Santa Fe salad and sweet tea, and went to the break room to eat it. Within the hour, I was fully dressed and standing behind the bar, sending Eugene down to have a break of his own.

By seven, the bar was packed, and Tank had a line-up waiting outside the door. That had never happened since I'd started working here. Good thing it wasn't raining.

The servers were so busy, I could hardly keep up with them. Thankfully, Eugene was manning the draft taps, making it easier for them to stay on top of their orders. His help kept things running smoothly, especially when he could work the bar while I introduced the acts.

Mercifully, while I hadn't seen Jack, he'd left the intros for me, along with an apology that had ended, *"I know you'll understand. Be happy, Andie. You deserve it."* He'd almost brought me to tears, but I did know how he felt, and I would soon be pulling a similar vanishing act of my own.

By ten-thirty, I was beat and more than a little disappointed since there had been no sign of Handsome Harry. I'd hoped he would show up, but that was a pipe dream. The third act had finished, and I'd just come back from a quick trip to the powder room when I saw him cross the floor and sit at the bar the way he had last night. My spirits soared. The man who'd occupied the seat had gone, only nursing a couple of drafts over the three hours that he'd been there, but he'd insisted on paying for each as he'd ordered them, almost as if he were waiting for someone or something. Whatever it was must've happened and he'd vacated the seat just in time for my favorite customer.

I hurried my steps. Eugene was on his way down the bar when I stopped him.

"I've got this. Go grab a few minutes of downtime. Everything looks to be under control for now."

"Thanks." The middle-aged man smiled. "I don't think the place has ever been this busy. Too bad the old man can't see it."

He stepped out from behind the bar, and I replaced him, grabbing a coaster as I hurried down to the seat at the end of the bar.

"Howdy, stranger. Fancy meeting you here again. What can I get ya?"

He grinned. "I told you I'd see you soon." His brow creased. "You did get my money and note?"

"I did and those General Grants were much appreciated. So what would you like? There's a local microbrewery draft on as tonight's special."

"That'll do."

I turned to leave.

"Wait, Andie. I know you don't know me from a hole in the ground, but I'm really a very nice guy."

My cheeks burned. I knew that about him and a whole lot more.

"Ya'll seem nice to me," I agreed.

"Then, how about joining me for dinner tomorrow night? There's this cute little Mexican place right next to my hotel."

I didn't wait to be asked again. I grabbed a card from the holder, scribbled my address and phone number, and handed it to him.

"I can be ready for six. Oh, and call if you change your mind."

He smiled. "I won't. I'll be there at six o'clock sharp."

"And I'll just go get that draft."

My feet wouldn't hurt when I got home tonight since I was now walking on air.

* * *

By the time I stepped onstage to make my last intro, I was dog-tired. Between making drinks for the waitresses and serving my own customers, the only conversation I'd had with LJ—I liked Handsome Harry better—had involved refilling his beer, not that the man was a heavy drinker.

I moved to the far side of the stage, knowing that Stan was right behind me. I could feel LJ's eyes on me, and they set my body on fire.

Tomorrow, tomorrow, I can't wait for tomorrow, it's less than a day away, my mind sang to *Annie's* iconic song.

The crowd quieted as they had each time I'd taken the stage tonight.

"Well, folks. Here we are at the final act of the evening before The Pickleback gets a makeover. As sad as I'll be to see this place change, I'm kinda excited to see the changes the new owners have in mind. Just remember, ya'll will be as welcome here as ya're now." I turned to the man making his way on stage, his large cat puppet cradled in his arms. "Some of you may recall Stan Masters and Wilson."

The room, as full as it had been all evening, broke out in applause. Stan, a ventriloquist with an orange tabby puppet, a cross between Garfield and the Internet famous Grumpy Cat, usually brought the house down.

"Evening, Stan. Hi, Wilson." I rubbed the puppet's head. "I've got a present for you, a little something I whipped up the other day 'specially for tonight." I handed him an envelope.

Stan reached for it, removing his hand from the puppet and pulled the sheet of paper out of the envelope. The eight by ten caricature showed Wilson standing on his back legs, with Stan on the puppet's resting place.

"This is incredible, Andie. I had no idea you were this talented." He held it up for the crowd to see. "Thank you. This means more than you'll ever know."

He leaned over and kissed my cheek. Afraid I was going to lose it and bawl like a baby, I started the routine for his introduction that we'd planned earlier.

"Knowing I was going to be introducing ya'll tonight, I brushed up on some cat jokes for Wilson."

Stan set the sketch down on the stool and replaced his hand inside the puppet. The cat straightened his head, stretching his neck a good four inches to bring his face closer to mine.

"You did that for me, luscious?" His eyebrows wiggled but not a muscle on Stan's face moved. "Lay them on me, Andie."

"Alright. Stan, what's a cat's favorite cocktail?"

Stan shook his head. "I don't know, Andie. What's a cat's favorite cocktail?"

"A Tom Cat Collins."

Wilson groaned loudly, drowning out some of the laughter.

"Listen sweetheart, stick to art. When it comes to cats, you don't know a thing about our drink preferences. Morley, the old tom who hangs out backstage at the strip club near the overpass, prefers Meowgaritas and Isabella, the pussy of my dreams, is partial to Fellini Pawseccos. She's always been an expensive date. I like six toed cats."

I cocked my head. "Isabella is polydactyl?"

The cat gave a very human-like shrug, "I don't know where she goes to church, and I don't care. Ever since Stan had me fixed last week, Isabella's been giving me the cold shoulder."

The crowd laughed.

"I'm sorry about that," I commiserated. "Polydactyl isn't a religion, it means to have an extra toe. You said you liked six-toed cats. I assumed—"

"Never assume and shake up that brain of yours, gorgeous. You'll injure yourself." The cat shook its head. "Now if you wanted to shake those tatas—I may not be human, but I'm male and breasts are breasts even if you only have two." The crowd roared. "Maybe it's time you consider a career change, because you aren't cutting it as a bartender."

I pretended to be affronted. "Why Wilson, that's a right mean thing to say. People think I'm doing a good job getting their drinks."

The crowd applauded with cries of "You're the best, honey."

"If you're so good, how come you can't make a Six Toed Cat?"

I cocked my head. "Are ya'll telling me that a Six Toed Cat is a cocktail? I've never heard of it."

"You need to get out of this place and travel more. I'm sure there's someone here who would love to spend a few days under the tropical sun teaching you a thing or two about cock … tails."

The crowd howled with comments of "I'm free," peppering the laughter.

I put my hands on my hips and stomped my foot, fighting to suppress my own giggles.

"Hush your mouth, you … mangy cat. How dare you? I'm not that kind of girl. My papa would whip you good for even thinking so."

"Too bad, but you can't blame a cat for trying. It's a drink named after Ernest Hemingway's six-toed cat, Snow White. It's made with Jamaican & Trinidadian rums, falernum, maraschino amaro, and grapefruit and cherry bitters. Garnish it with a little catnip, and I'll be your love slave." The puppet moved closer and laid his head on my arm. "It's been a rough week."

Stan looked at the cat. "I thought you were off alcohol since your surgery?"

The cat puppet raised his head and seemed to glare at Stan.

"No thanks to you," Wilson sneered. "You've got an eye for the ladies, but I don't see you getting fixed."

"But I'm not the one who went out tomcatting and came home with one foot in the grave."

"It was only one foot, and I have nine lives. They're going to be damn boring ones from now on—no pussy, no fighting, the least I can do is drink."

The cat pulled his head in and sighed.

"I'm plum sorry about your … operation," I smiled, "but isn't that cocktail a little strong for a cat your size?"

"You know nothing about my size," he groaned, "but from now one, it's the only kind of tail I'm ever going to get." He lifted his back leg in search of what the doctor had snipped off. "They were majestic balls. Thanks for nothing, Stan."

I laughed along with the crowd. "Ladies and gents, give it up for Stan and Wilson."

Returning to my bar duties, I listened to the banter between the man and his puppet as I served my chairs and made cocktails for the other servers.

I stopped at the end of the bar to refill LJ's draft.

"You really do have a knack for comedy, but I had no idea you were an artist."

I chuckled. "Artist might be a bit of a stretch. I draw some, make caricatures like that one tonight, and work a bit with oils and pastels. I'm right proud of the sunset I painted while sitting on Venice Beach. That's one of my favorite spots in LA."

"I hope you'll show it to me."

"You'll see it when you pick me up tomorrow night. Now, this gal has to git back to work."

As always, the comedian and his puppet put on a great show. When they finished, the DJ went into his last set, and the crowd started to thin.

LJ signaled to me, and I went along the bar to see what he wanted.

"I've got to go." He handed me two twenties.

"That's way too much," I argued, trying to hand back one of the bills.

"Keep it. Consider it payment for the entertainment. I'll see you…" he glanced at his watch and grinned, "Tonight."

I nodded and smiled. "I'll be waiting."

I'd just rung up the sale and put the extra twenty plus the change from the first one into my tip jar when Stan, minus Wilson, approached the bar and took one of the recently vacated seats.

"Thanks again for the caricature, Andie. You pretty well summed up the act. The cat has always been in charge. You do know I was only joking about your abilities."

I handed him the beer he usually had after the show. "Course I do. Besides, in the last hour I actually made more than a dozen of those cocktails. It's amazing what ya'll can learn on the Internet if ya know what you're looking for."

He nodded. "My wife drank those when we used to go to the Caribbean on vacation. We lived in New Jersey back then, and while she grew to love California, she missed the snow. She was also a big Hemingway fan." He picked up the mug. "I'm going to miss you and this place. That was my last show. Wilson and I are retiring. Jack's right. There comes a time when a man has to consider how much time he's got left."

I stopped wiping the bar, reminded once more of my own father's age.

"Why? You aren't that old, and you know the crowd loves you. You'd be welcome here any night."

He shook his head once more. "You may be right, but it wouldn't be the same. I've been thinking of going home for some time now. I probably would've left sooner if it hadn't been for Jack. My son wants me to move back to Trenton. He and his wife just had a new baby, and with Effie gone and Jack moving to Alaska, there's nothing keeping me here."

I smiled. "I envy you. Grandbabies win out over rowdy drunks any day."

He laughed. "When are you going to settle down and start a family of your own? There must be someone back in Texas waiting for grandchildren."

I looked down at the counter so as not to meet his eyes. I was tired of lying about who and what I was. It wasn't fair to people like Stan and Jess. Was it fair to LJ? But that was different.

"My siblings are looking after that. When do you leave?"

"Next week. The van will be here to pack up on Monday. I've already decided what I want to keep. Don't sell yourself short, Andie. I'm sure your family cares for you as much as they do your siblings. I can see gorgeous, deep blue-eyed babies in your future. It's sure to be a good one, especially if you get out of here and focus on your art. You're a great comedian, but most people can tell a joke, but draw like this?" He held up the envelope. "That's a God-given gift."

He handed me twenty bucks.

"Stan, you know the beer's on the house."

"Yeah, but the tip isn't. That's for you."

"And I hope you have a wonderful time with your son and that grandbaby."

He drained his beer, set the mug on the bar, and walked away.

I blinked to keep my eyes from filling with tears. I'd always hated goodbyes, and suddenly I was saying far too many of them.

It was almost two when I locked the bar receipts in the safe for the last time and used my cell phone to call my UBER.

"Not a bad way to finish, Tank. Sales were good tonight. A great going away bonus for Jack."

"Yeah. I'm going to miss working here. I wasn't crazy about it when I started, took a while to get used to the hours, but…"

"Aren't you coming back?"

He shrugged. "Not sure. It's all up in the air right now. It'll depend on the boss."

"I'm sure even upscale places need bouncers; they just call them doormen. When do you turn in the keys?"

"I don't. Jack told me to keep them as a souvenir. I noticed a few people left with a piece of the place themselves. I was told to let them. Did you grab anything?"

"Yeah. I took a Pickleback shot glass. As far as the keys go, it makes sense that the new owner won't want to run the risk of having extra keys running around."

Phil honked the horn.

I turned back to Tank. "Maybe I'll see you in September."

He grinned. "If you'll be here, then so will I. Enjoy your summer, Andie."

"You, too."

CHAPTER TEN

Despite not getting to bed before three, I was up at nine. I'd tossed and turned like a slab of pizza dough twirled in the air by an Italian chef. When I finally accepted that further sleep would be impossible, I got up, grabbed my phone, and made a few calls. By ten o'clock, dressed in my best slacks, a fashionable top, and low-heeled sandals, I called a cab and headed downtown.

Valentina's was the hairdresser Kelly had recommended, and I'd been using her for the last five months to keep the style and color Shangri-la felt suited me best. After a trim and a color lift, I walked next door to the nail salon for a pedicure and a manicure, something I'd treated myself to all along. Nails polished a soft pink, a color that would match anything, I started my search for something to wear specifically for tonight. I might've preferred something from the shops on Rodeo Drive, stores Andressa Myers had frequented when in LA, but if LJ hadn't recognized me, neither would they. The last time I'd tried to shop there, looking for a suitable baby gift for Ingrid, I'd been treated to the same snobbery as Vivian in *Pretty Woman*, without the benefit of Edward there to grease palms. Learning the extent of the dichotomy between the wealthy and the rest of society had been an eye opener. In the end, I'd gone downtown and had purchased a gift for Ingrid's son from a sweet, little boutique that specialized in children's clothing.

Now, not wanting a bad experience to ruin my day, I headed for a store that sold discounted designer clothes. Sure, they were a season or two out of vogue, but did that really matter? I doubted LJ knew what was on the Paris runways any more than I did. Giving the matter a lot of thought, I selected a black, mini dress that would be perfect for almost any occasion, showed off my cleavage, and cinched my waist. I paired it with wedge-heeled black sandals. On a whim, I went into a lingerie store and bought three new sets of bras and panties. If things worked out … As far as jewelry went, I bought some funky silver and turquoise hoops from a Native American street vendor.

It was almost four by the time I made it home.

When I got out of the cab, Mrs. Richards called to me.

"Andie, I have a delivery for you." She went inside her house and came out with a small bouquet of roses, six gorgeous yellow ones.

"They're beautiful," I exclaimed, reaching for the card.

No one had ever sent me flowers before.

The card read, *For my Texas rose*, and was signed, *LJ*.

Hadn't I thought him perfect?

I looped the bag handles around my wrist and reached for the vase.

"It's from my dinner date," I admitted.

Mrs. Richards smiled. "I may not know much about men, but I know a keeper when I see one."

I grinned. "He is rather special."

"Well, any man who can light up your eyes like that has to be. You have a great evening."

"I'm sure I will."

I carried the roses upstairs, put then down on the veranda long enough to unlock the door, and then brought them inside, placing them on the breakfast bar.

Exhaling heavily, I let the reality of what was happening fill me. I had a date with Handsome Harry, the *real* man I'd fantasized about for the last nine months, a man who'd captured my heart the moment he'd massaged my foot. Was I crazy? Probably. Was I putting the cart before the horse? Definitely, but this was my one and only chance to grasp the brass ring and achieve my dreams. I wasn't asking for much. If LJ fell in love with me before I admitted who I was, if he agreed to marry me before I told him the size of my bank account, and if he accepted that our lives were back in Texas at Quaternity where I was the vet, then my life would be absolutely perfect.

In the back of my mind, I heard Mama's words. *"Andie, darling. You're much too hard on yourself. You must remember, perfect is often the enemy of good, and sometimes good is what we really need."*

I sobered. Had I done it again? Had I striven for perfection when good would've been enough? No. I couldn't go there now. What was done was done. Tonight, I would be with the man of my dreams.

While I hadn't dated a lot over the years, my name and background, not to mention Daddy's security men and women shadowing me wherever I went, had made getting picked up in a coffee shop, in a bar, or even in church on Sunday almost impossible. I'd managed to meet a few acceptable men at university, men whose father's bank accounts rivaled my own, spoiled entitled men who were as exciting and interesting as dishwater. I'd left my virginity in Simon Lovatt's dorm room in my sophomore year, an event unworthy of a footnote in history. Simon had gone on to date and eventually marry my far more attractive classmate Vanessa Morgan. After that less than stellar activity, dating had been sporadic at best.

After graduation and before returning to Quaternity, I'd suffered through a couple of blind dates Ingrid had initiated. She'd already met Will, and the men she set me up with were also cosmetic surgeons. Sadly, the conversation had centered around what they considered the ideals of beauty, the recommended breast size for their patients, or why I would want to be a vet when my family had all that money, and I could do whatever I wanted. They just didn't understand that I needed to be me, to do something with my life that mattered.

Once I'd returned to the ranch, my father between wives as it were, I'd been his hostess, occasionally accepting a dinner invitation from one of his colleagues, but I hated that lifestyle, and I'd been self-conscious of my appearance. Daddy had gone away to a business meeting in Pittsburg and had come back with Becki, the latest Mrs. Myers, who'd taken my place, sparing me those ordeals. I'd been able to focus on the animals—until my twenty-fifth birthday.

Since I'd settled into this charade, I'd actually dated more often than I ever had before, although I'd avoided intimacy most of the time. As I'd told Wilson, the cat puppet, I didn't sleep around. Some of those dates had been dismal failures, others not so bad. Determined to find Mr. Right and prove to my father and sisters that I could find true love on my own, I'd opened myself up to the new experience.

My first venture into the LA dating scene had been with Devin. I'd met him shortly after I'd started at The Pickleback when he'd come into the bar to drop off the keys to Jack's antique 1957 Ford Fairlane he'd repaired. He'd been a little disheveled and let's face it, downright dirty, with grease and oil stained jeans, a muscle shirt that might've been bleached a year ago, and a red bandana covering what I later learned was a balding head. He'd tied back his long, stringy hair and was in need of a shave, but he'd been charming. After he'd finished his free beer, he'd invited me to join him and a few friends for a day at the beach and a barbecue. Reasoning that he'd just come from the garage and was bound to clean up nicely, I'd accepted. He was every inch the bad boy I'd read about in trashy novels the girls had hidden under their mattresses at boarding school, and I was lonely. I'd mentioned it to Jack. While the man hadn't told me not to go, I could tell he was concerned. He gave me his cell number and told me to call if I needed anything. As it turned out, I did.

Sunday morning, after spending time on my hair and my outfit—jeans as he'd suggested, a long-sleeved, cotton blouse over a red tank top, and my cowboy boots—I'd slathered on the special sunscreen Will had given me. I was ready when Devin hollered my name at the top of his voice, tacking on, "I'm waiting."

Slightly annoyed, I grabbed my bag containing a simple blue maillot, a towel, and my sunhat, locked the door, and hurried down the stairs. Devin sat astride a Harley at the end of the driveway. I was surprised to see he looked no different than he had earlier in the week. The man hadn't shaved … I doubted he'd showered either, and appeared to wear the same outfit he had before, the only difference being a jean jacket with the sleeves ripped off and mirrored sunglasses. Seeing him like that, I almost backed out, pleading a migraine, when I stopped myself. I was judging a man solely on his appearance. Hadn't I wanted a man who worked for a living? The grease under his fingernails proved that he did. Maybe he'd had an unexpected emergency to deal with. The last thing I wanted to do was let my snobbery shine through.

He lowered his sunglasses and eyed me up and down, the way a starving dog might look at a tomahawk steak in a butcher shop window.

"Looking good, babe. The guys are going to beg for some of what I'll get later."

He winked, leading naïve me to believe he was joking. He wasn't, but his expectations bore no fruit.

I might've been comfortable on horseback, but I'd never been on a motorcycle. When I told him that, he just laughed.

"You'll get the hang of it in no time, Texas. You can ride a horse and a man, can't you? Just spread your legs wide the way you would in a saddle. There's not much of a difference. Now, step on the pedal, swing a leg over, slide that cute little butt of yours down until you're cupping my ass, and then hold on. You'll love it. Play your cards right, and there's an orgasm in every ride."

I smiled. "Who wouldn't want that?"

Thankfully, he had a helmet for me, and sitting close enough to feel his body heat leaching through his clothing, I hung on for dear life as we wove in and out of LA traffic until we reached the freeway, getting off at one of the exits that led to a coastal road. It didn't take long for me to get my seat, and once I did, I slid back a little, relaxing in the fresher air and the thrill of the ride, wishing the man in front of me smelled slightly spicy instead of pungent.

Within the hour, we pulled off the road at a secluded beach. There were already almost two dozen bikers there, some with girls of their own. Most of the riders were part of the same gang Devin was, the patches on their jackets and vests depicting skeletons on motorcycles slaughtering pigs, the words *Knights of the Road* written in red. I might've led a sheltered life, but I got the symbolism. Most of the men and women used four letter words as articles to qualify everything else they said. A few could've used a good mouth-washing since they didn't seem acquainted with toothpaste and mouthwash. To make matters worse, they were gropy, a little too free with their hands on any female body that came near them. If you wanted to grab my ass, you should at least say please.

These guys might've considered themselves the knights of the road, but they were a far cry from knights in shining armor. They were rude, crude, and downright ornery, and Devin was the worst of the lot, acting as if he'd done me a huge favor by making me his bitch for the day.

Shortly after we arrived, I went with the other women to change into my suit, our private change room nothing more than a clump of boulders. My suit covered a whole lot more of me than any of theirs did. Going out again, I was embarrassed by Devin's loud guffaws.

"Where in hell did you get that thing? From a convent?"

"Actually, ya'll, it's a competition suit. I used to swim competitively."

"Well, ya'll," one of the others mocked. "This ain't no swim meet."

Most of the men, including Devin, stripped naked to swim. I did my best to avert my eyes, but I soon realized that all men were not created equal, and God's gifts were dispersed haphazardly. Devin was well-endowed and seemed to enjoy being admired by men and women alike. Some of the women joined in their back to nature swimming. I wasn't one of them, much to Devin's displeasure.

The only consolation to the sun-worshiping swimmers was that a few of them smelled better after a dip in the ocean since many of the men and a few of the women only seemed to have a cursory knowledge of basic hygiene.

I wasn't by any means a feminist, but I balked at the way those men ordered the women around, expecting to be waited on like kings, not the jackasses they were, sitting there as naked as Adam in the garden, drinking beer, smoking and toking joints, and cursing the establishment.

While in Texas, grilling is a man's forte, on that beach, the women did all the work, and when it was time to eat, the men descended on the food like pigs at a trough. Even Prince Leopold and Jackson had shown more class than them. Okay, maybe my background was making me overly sensitive, but I was dang sure that the entire day was a waste of time. I wasn't going to find my soulmate or any other kind of mate here. By mid-afternoon, I was definitely not going to go back into the city on the back of that bike.

Devin and a few of the others passed out in the sun, and I took the opportunity to pull on my jeans and shirt, grab my bag, and head back up the road. We'd passed a gas station a short distance back, and I headed there to phone Jack. If ever I needed a white knight, it was then and there. Jack had come for me, and he hadn't said a word about it, no "I warned you," or "I told you so." He'd just driven me home and dropped me off, with a "See you at work on Wednesday."

A few days later, Devin popped into the bar. He'd wondered what had happened to me that day. Obviously, he hadn't worried too hard. When he asked if I wanted to join him for a sunset ride to pick up where we'd left off, I demurred.

He'd shrugged. "Your loss, Texas, your loss."

Learning a valuable lesson that day, I'd been more careful about the men I chose to date. I was looking for my ideal man, not just any man. I could afford to be picky. I'd gone out with Lou, the bar's resident DJ, a couple of times. He'd been the one to take me to Venice Beach. The artisan area had appealed to me. After seeing me doodle on a napkin, the image being that of a pelican and a sea gull fighting over a fish, he'd encouraged me to draw caricatures. The next time we'd gone out there, he'd gifted me with a sketch pad and charcoal pencils. I'd drawn one of him snoozing in the sun, that had led to my drawing some for cash—ten-dollar souvenirs. We'd had fun, but there'd been no magic, no sparks, no fire between us. We'd remained friends. Like Jess and Tank, I would miss him was the charade was over.

I'd had a few lackluster dates after Lou, including Carson, a Ph D student at UCLA working on a degree in neuroscience. The man came into the bar on a daily basis, watched a couple of acts, made notes, and then left, always leaving a five-dollar tip on the bar. He was attractive enough, and definitely smart, but his field of study was the only thing he could discuss, and to someone with little interest in the physical workings of the brain, it grew wearisome. After a few too many tequila shots, we'd made it to the bedroom, but while the man's performance had been exemplary, he couldn't stop quizzing me about how I felt before, during, and after. It occurred to me that I'd been nothing more than an extension of his bar experiment to him.

After a few dismal dates with men whose shoe size might actually have equaled their IQ, and whose conversation was limited to how much they could lift at the gym, I met Randy. He was perfect in every way—tall, blond, hazel-eyed, with facial scruff that had reminded me of Handsome Harry. I was smitten. Here was my answer to prayer, the man I could marry. A salesman for one of the bar's liquor suppliers, he was only in LA on Wednesday and Thursday, and we didn't waste a minute of our time together. He wasn't a selfish lover, but he didn't spend much time making sure I was as satisfied as he was. Since orgasms weren't really in my vocabulary, I chose to overlook that side of our relationship. I was in love, and it was marvelous— most of the time. When he professed his undying love for me, hinting that a walk down the aisle might be in our future, I thought, he's the one.

Unfortunately, Fate rained on that parade a few weeks later when Jess persuaded me to join her sister and brother-in-law at Disneyland. We were waiting for the kids to get off the Pirates of the Caribbean ride when I saw him and pointed him out to Jess. I stood and headed toward him, stopped in my tracks by a pregnant woman rushing in the same direction, holding a young girl by one hand and a slightly older boy by the other, the children's screams of "Daddy, Daddy, Daddy!" completing the picture I'd never wanted to see. I ducked behind a souvenir stand and watched him embrace the woman and his children. Like that day in the dining room, my temper boiled over, but before I could ruin a family forever, Jess pulled me away, calming me enough for me to realize that if I said something, I would be leaving the woman and her two children, soon to be three, alone without a means of support. Jess consoled me that night. She thought I was crying over a broken heart. I was crying over a broken dream.

The next time he came into the bar, expecting me to jump into his bed in his motel room on Sunset Boulevard, Jess and I confronted him. He tried to lie his way out of it, claiming that woman was his sister. Fool that I was, still in pain and reeling from it, I wanted to give him the benefit of the doubt. Jess, more levelheaded than I was, insisted he call her and have her come down to the bar and join him for dinner on her. He made all kinds of excuses, some plausible, others stinking more than the midden at noon on a summer's day. When she refused to back down, it had all come apart, and the truth, or rather some variation of it had come spilling out.

The following week, a new liquor rep had shown up, explaining that with Randy's wife so close to her due date, he'd switched his territory to the San Francisco area to be closer to home. I hoped the man had learned his lesson, but I doubted it. A leopard didn't change his spots.

After that disgusting display of gullibility on my part, I'd been pickier than ever. I shook myself. Enough of dwelling on failure. Throughout the months since my birthday, I'd thought of Handsome Harry, and unknowingly, had set an impossible, idealistic standard of the right man for me. I'd created this paragon based on ten minutes of conversation and a foot massage. No wonder I'd been willing to fall for a Casanova like Randy, a poor facsimile of the man who'd fascinated me. Well, I'd found him now, and I intended to see him fall in love with me. I had two months to do it, so why was I wasting time revisiting my failures?

Every campaign needed a plan. The first step in that plan was to make sure I left him wanting more. Tonight, I intended to get to know him, his likes and dislikes, and what he was like as a person. There was always a slim chance that the image I had of him was a false one, after all, he'd been paid to work there that night, paid to be nice to the guest, paid to be nice to me. I shrugged that off. No. The man was more than a sycophant, trying to please the person at the other end of his paycheck. LJ was courteous, thoughtful, and had a good sense of humor—and gave great foot massages.

I grabbed a bottle of water from the kitchen before going into the bathroom to shave my legs and armpits and trim my bush. It hadn't been waxed in months, but I'd kept the growth under control. I wasn't very hairy to begin with.

When I finished, I showered, careful not to wet my hair. Afterward, I donned one of my new bra and panty sets, and then returned to the bathroom to do my makeup. Finally, I spritzed myself with the perfume I'd brought with me from home, the perfume I'd worn on my birthday. It was a gutsy move. If it triggered his memory, and he recalled who I was, I wouldn't lie to him. I would admit everything and hope for the best; if it didn't, I would carry out my plan to make him fall in love with me and wait until he was head over heels, ready to pop the question, to tell him the truth.

Going into my bedroom, I removed the tags from the dress and slipped it over my head. In the past five months, I'd not only kept those twenty pounds off, but I'd also lost another five and looked good even if I did say so myself.

Returning to the living room, I checked the cleanliness of the place. More than passable. I turned on the TV and sat down to wait. I did say I would be ready, and I was.

At five to six, someone knocked at the door. Praying it was LJ and not my landlady, I hurried to answer it.

My prayers were answered. He wore an ivory golf shirt and khaki slacks, his feet incased in leather slip-ons.

"Wow, you look fantastic." The appreciation in his eyes proved his words.

"Thank you, kind sir. You don't look so bad yourself. Come on in. Have we got time for a drink? I don't have a wide selection, but I've got beer."

"Beer's fine by me."

He stepped inside.

"Have a seat. I'll get the beer. Oh, and that's the painting I mentioned last night." I indicated the landscape on the far side of the room.

Ignoring the sofa, he walked over to the wall, examining my art work.

When I came back with two glasses of beer, he'd taken a seat. I handed him a glass before sitting next to him.

"Thanks." He took a mouthful and then used his glass to point to the painting. "That's incredible. You are an amazingly talented woman, Andie Harper."

My cheeks burned. At the compliment or at the use of my false name? This was no time to be getting cold feet.

I swallowed a mouthful of beer. "Thank ya, kind suhh," I answered, not quite ready to ditch my disguise. "And thank you for the gorgeous yellow roses. How'd ya'll know they were my favorite?"

"I didn't," he chuckled. "I wanted to send you bluebonnets, which I read were Texas's official state flower, but the florist didn't have any. He said yellow roses were associated with Austin, the capital, so I hoped they would do."

I nodded. "They'll do very nicely, thank you, although bluebonnets do run a close second in my heart. My mama loved those. They grow wild on the ranch—the one my daddy worked on when I was growing up."

I'd almost put my foot in it, revealing more than I should have. Not wanting to risk being asked about the ranch or Mama, knowing she wouldn't condone this deception despite the purity of my motives, I changed the subject.

"Have ya'll figured out how long you'll be in LA?"

"At least until the end of September." He put down his glass and stood. "Andie, I have a confession to make."

I swallowed. Here it was. He was about to tell me he knew who I was. Could I be as honest?

"I'm…" he began, staring into my eyes.

Could he see my fear, my sorrow, or my guilt written there? My heart thudded in my chest, my pulse no doubt visible in my neck.

He shook his head. "My name is Lee James. I'm the new manager of The Pickleback."

I blinked, the sense of relief making me weak. I was expecting something far worse.

"Say something," he begged.

I opened my mouth, not sure I could speak. "Why didn't you tell me yesterday or the day before?" I croaked.

"Because I was afraid you wouldn't go out with me if you knew."

I scowled. "Why? I don't see … Oh!" My eyes opened wide. "Does Mr. Rayburn frown on his employees dating each other?"

Sleeping with the boss might not be a good idea, but he wouldn't officially be my boss until Labor Day when The Pickleback reopened. A lot could happen in two months. We could fall in love, marry in Vegas, and then, when I told him the truth … No, I would have to tell him before the marriage if I wanted it to be legal.

He shook his head. "Not as far as I know; I just thought you might."

I grinned. "Well, since this is only dinner, why don't we worry about the boss-employee thing later? After all, technically you won't be until the bar reopens." I finished my beer. "Are we ready?"

He nodded. "I like the way you think." He drained his glass. "And we are. Let's see what tonight brings and worry about the future tomorrow."

I went into my bedroom to get my shoes and purse. I couldn't help thinking he still had something on his mind, something he was reluctant to share, and since I had secrets of my own, he was entitled to his.

Mañana.

I would worry about it tomorrow.

CHAPTER ELEVEN

The Mexican restaurant, Casa Del Oro, was a quaint place in Inglewood. From the outside, it looked like a typical adobe building, but inside the décor with its lush plants, indoor waterfall, and wicker furniture, made you feel as though you were outside in the courtyard of a hacienda on a warm summer's night.

After the hostess showed us to our table, a nice private one near the indoor fountain, I turned to LJ.

"What should I call you? The other night when you introduced yourself, you told me your name was LJ, but tonight you said it was Lee." I chewed my lower lip. "I like that better than initials."

He grinned. "So do I, but you can call me whatever you like."

"Then, Lee it is." I smiled. The man was full of surprises. "Have you been here before?"

Nodding, he reached for the water glass on the table.

"I have. It's one of my favorite restaurants in LA. I like quiet, out-of-the-way places. It's great to hobnob with celebrities, but sometimes, it's nice to find a place that can mean something special to you."

"Do you spend a lot of time in LA?"

He shook his head, his eyes clouding. "I did as a kid, before my parents died." He indicated the menu. "Everything is good. Order your favorites. You won't be disappointed."

Knowing better than to pry on something that was obviously a sensitive topic, I shrugged. "I haven't had all that much Mexican food—I mean Tex-Mex, sure but that's not the same as authentic Mexican cuisine like the sign says." The truth was I'd only been to Mexico a few times, and what food

I'd eaten had been whatever was served at the banquets I'd attended. "What would you recommend?"

"Why don't you let me order and surprise you? We can start with house margaritas and go from there?"

"Sounds good."

So far, he was exceeding all expectations.

When the waiter came over, he ordered in flawless Spanish, a language I knew well. You couldn't live in Texas without picking it up.

Making conversation, I smiled. "Your Spanish is amazing. Where did you learn to speak it so well?"

Once more, he reached for his water glass.

"Back in university, I got a summer job working at a vineyard in California, just outside of San Francisco. Most of the workers spoke Spanish. I'd done quite well with it in school … By the time I went back to Penn State, I'd improved. Since then, I've kept it up. Do you?"

"*Un poco*," I lied, playing up the Texas accent. "So, ya'll went to Penn State. I hear that's one of the big schools." And one with steep tuitions costs. "Were you there on a sports' scholarship?"

He shook his head. "I used to play ball, but I got injured and stopped playing in my early teens."

"Oh, I'm sorry. I had to quit competitive swimming when I was twelve because of asthma." I reached for my own water glass, well aware that I might've given him too much information. "What was your major?"

"Finance, with an emphasis on the hospitality industry. What about you?"

"Community college," I lied once more. It was really only a white lie. Ithaca was a community. "Vet technician. I like working with animals."

"Then why are you tending bar in LA?"

I swallowed, reminded of Kelly's admonition to stay as close to the truth as possible.

"The last animal I looked after died. I blamed myself. Someone once told me we all come to LA for different reasons. Getting away from the pain was one of mine. As for working as a bartender, I enjoy it."

I was saved from saying any more by the arrival of our margaritas. I'd made many of those tequila-based drinks, but this rivaled my best attempt.

"These are fantastic. I should ask the bartender for the recipe, although a lot of them keep their individual mixes a secret."

"I'm sure if you bat those pretty blue eyes, he'd tell you."

I laughed. "I don't bat my eyes, silly. No one can do that. I bat my eyelids." I demonstrated. "Did it work?" He nodded. "Now, tell me all your secrets."

Lee chuckled. "Andie, your wish is my command. What would you like to know?"

"Everything."

The waiter returned with ceviche and tortilla chips. I'd had both before, but these were exquisite. We'd just finished the margaritas when he brought over a large pitcher of red sangria to accompany the chalupa appetizers.

As we ate, we discussed our musical preferences, our favorite movies, debated which Marvel hero was the greatest, and agreed that the latest Star Trek franchises were the best. I avoided personal questions that might require similar answers from me. I did want to know everything, but I didn't want to give away my own secrets yet.

He asked about my art, questioned why I'd never pursued it as a career, not satisfied when I'd answered that there really wasn't any money in it. I'd won a couple of competitions in high school, but since I'd opted to fast track my degree in veterinary medicine, there hadn't been time for further study.

The second course was a traditional soup with a red chili base. The menudo was delicious and while I wasn't normally fond of tripe, I cleaned my bowl. The entrée followed the soup course. The Pescado Zarendeado, a white fish dish where the meat was roasted over a mangrove-wood grill called a zaranda, was served with lemon and chili sauce.

The fish melted in my mouth. The last course, dessert, consisted of an orange-scented flan and churros.

I pushed away my plate. "I can't eat another bite. That was probably more food than I've eaten at one time in months, but it was delicious. Thank you."

He reached for the second pitcher of sangria he'd ordered earlier and emptied it into first my glass and then his.

"It's not just the food," he stated. "It's the company. I haven't enjoyed a meal this much in a long time."

Leaning back in the chair, I reached for my glass and sipped. I didn't need any more wine. I had just the right amount of buzz on, but it was delicious.

Wanting to know more about him, I picked up the conversation we'd started earlier.

"I agree. Both the meal and the company were great. Tell me, how long have you worked for Rayburn Enterprises?"

He sipped his wine, something he seemed to do before he answered any questions, almost as if he was using the action to organize his thoughts. I smothered a giggle. A man who thought before he spoke. What a novel idea.

"Officially? About a year. I started learning the ropes before that. My family has worked for them for years. You might say it's in my blood."

I frowned. "A year ago? Then how come—"

I stopped. The wine had loosened my tongue. I'd been about to ask why he'd been working for the caterer on my birthday.

He narrowed his eyes slightly. "How come what?"

I scrambled for an answer. "That's not a long time. How come they made you the manager of The Pickleback? Jack said it was part of a new project or something, so it must be important."

He grinned. "I guess I've proven my worth, but it's just a temporary position."

The band started to play "Guantanamera," a song I loved.

"Would you like to dance?"

I'd dreamed of dancing with him instead of Prince Leopold. How could I possibly pass up a chance to be in his arms? I nodded.

He stood and reached out his hand.

Without a word, I got to my feet, put my hand in his, and let him lead me to the dance floor. As I'd suspected, he was an excellent dancer, holding me tight, but not too tight. Despite the difference in height, we fit together as if we were meant to be that way. Our heartbeats melded, thudding slowly to the sound of the music. He didn't speak, didn't try to sing the lyrics to the song, although I'd wager, he would know the right words. We glided across the floor seamlessly, and when the song ended, he led me back to the table, his hand at the base of my spine filling me with heat.

"My hotel is nearby." His voice was husky. "Would you like to come up to my room for a nightcap?"

The plan was to leave him wanting more, but at that moment, I was the one who wanted more, needed more, so much more. The clock was ticking. It was time for a leap of faith.

"I'd like that." I smiled shyly, hoping he wanted more than to share a drink.

He called for the check, paid the bill, and escorted me outside where a cab waited. I'd been about to suggest an UBER, since cabs weren't always easy to find at this time of night. Perhaps Fate was on my side this time.

His hotel wasn't exactly nearby. The four-star Hilton was a great place to stay, not as expensive as some, but close to The Pickleback. He would need an apartment soon since hotel accommodations weren't cheap. Of course, Rayburn Enterprises was probably footing the bill.

As soon as we stepped into the elevator, my nerves took over.

"How long are you going to stay here? Will you look for an apartment?"

He shook his head. "Probably not. I told you I'd be leaving at the end of September. My job is to see to the renovations, get the club up and running, and then appoint a manager to look after it from then on, reporting to me. I'll probably select one of the staff. Are you interested in applying for the job?"

Since I would be leaving then myself, hopefully with him by my side, I shook my head.

"No, thanks. I'm happy where I am, but why would the new manager report to you? Why not to Cole Rayburn or some Board of Directors?"

He put his arm around me. "That's just the way it is. They report to me, and I report to the Board."

I nodded. "Makes sense. He can't be looking after every little detail personally. What's he like?"

The elevator dinged, and the doors slid open.

"He's a nice guy, cares about people, doesn't like a lot of fuss. He's meticulous, does his own research, and won't let anyone railroad him into something he doesn't want to do. I suppose you could say he's his own man. This is our floor. Not the penthouse, but the view is spectacular."

He held my hand as we walked along the hallway to a corner room that turned out to be a small suite.

I went to stand by the window in what was the living room section.

"What would you like?" He opened the bar fridge. "We've got Amaretto, Grand Marnier, Cognac, wine, beer, or pop—no, let me take that back. You call every non-alcoholic, gassy drink, coke."

I laughed. "We do, but I'll take a Grand Marnier, straight if you don't have ice."

"There's an ice machine around here somewhere, but I haven't made its acquaintance."

I shook my head. "Now, who's the funny one?"

He handed me the drink.

I sipped, feeling the orange burn raise my temperature higher than it already was.

"Delicious."

He raised his own glass in a toast. "Here's to many more dinners together."

And nights.

I sipped once more before pivoting to look out the window, my gaze focusing on the lights below us and those in the distance. Somehow, it made me feel small and vulnerable. In the window's reflection, I saw him step closer to me.

Turning once more, I smiled. "I don't know what all to say about Mr. Rayburn, but he certainly treats his employees well. I suppose since you're here for three months, you deserve some perks, and this is a mighty fine one."

He nodded, moving to stand closer to me, the heat in his eyes making me smoulder. Nervously, I finished my drink. Time to leave.

"Thanks. That hit the spot." I licked my lips, drawing his attention to them. Setting down the glass, I moved a fraction away. "I should get going." Was that gruff voice mine? "I'll get a cab downstairs."

"Stay." His word echoed Edward's, but unlike Vivian, I nodded.

Placing his empty glass next to mine, he pulled me tightly to him. His gaze met mine, its question unmistakable. I knew what he wanted. I wanted it, too.

"The only perk I need is you," he whispered, before fastening his mouth on mine.

I'd dreamed of this kiss for months, fantasised about being in his arms like this, but never in my wildest dreams had I come close to the reality of it. His lips were soft, gentle, and yet masterful. When his tongue licked at mine, I opened to him, taking it within my mouth, savoring its touch, its texture, its taste. Had he not been holding me, I would've collapsed, turning to molten lava, and setting fire to everything around me.

Every part of me was ablaze as I felt more alive than I ever had, more desirable than I'd ever felt, and more fulfilled than I'd ever expected to be.

I couldn't tell you how or when it started, but soon we were moving into the bedroom leaving a trail of garments behind us.

Then, he released my mouth. I almost begged him to take it again, but the burning in his eyes told me that he had other plans. We stood at the side of the bed, now wearing nothing but our underwear. He lay me in the center of the bed, slowly divested me and himself of our last vestiges of clothing, and then lay on his side beside me. I wanted to ask him to turn off the lights, but he'd probably see it as false modesty. I was a modern woman, one who'd wrestled to bitches to the ground and had won.

He pulled me into his arms, finding my mouth once more. Within seconds, the fantasies I'd created over the months became the only reality that mattered. His hands moved over my skin, blazing a trail with his touch. He pulled his mouth away from mine and kissed his way down to my new breasts, laving the thin, barely-there scar from the augmentation. If he said anything, I would fess up to the surgery. Lots of women improved on Mother Nature. I'd simply done my part. His hands kneaded as his mouth suckled, tightening the spring within me one delicious lick after another.

Gently, while he continued to suckle, he moved his hands down my belly, rubbing my taut stomach, making his way to my mound. Once there, he pressed one finger between my labia, then another, teasing the swollen flesh with a touch as light as a butterfly's kiss. One finger slipped lower, and I shuddered. When a second found its way into my wet core, I bucked with all the strength of a bronc. I didn't want him to stop. I wanted more.

My arms reached for him, my hands momentarily arrested by the skin on his back, all puckered and ridged. Was that a remnant of the accident he'd mentioned? I continued my exploration, my fingers tangling in the golden curls on his chest, my hands moving down his washboard abs, stopping just short of his penis. Was I brazen enough to touch its velvety hardness?

Another finger entered me, and the decision was made. I moaned, gripping his penis, running my hand up and down its length, stopping only long enough to rub a gout of his juices across its top.

Oh God! Nothing had ever felt like this, certainly not the fumbling attempts of the few men I'd indulged myself with, nor the occasional encounters with my dildo. With his fingers filling me, pushing in, pulling out, turning and teasing, I almost flew off the bed when his thumb found my nub and rubbed harder and harder. There was no me. My body had become an extension of my pussy, getting the kind of adoration every woman dreamed of. My head flopped from side to side as I enjoyed the exquisite coiling inside me created by the movement of those expert fingers. I raised my hips, pushing against his hand, wanting to increase the marvelous ecstasy filling me.

My nerves tensed; my body was primed and ready for the mysterious and magical something that had eluded me before. He didn't stop his ministrations, rather increasing them, and I flew apart, carried on wave after wave of intense sensation. He slowed his movements, pulling his hand away as my vagina pulsed. I was still riding the wave when he plunged into me. My body clenched around him as he pumped, first slowly, going deep and almost pulling all the way out, and then faster, deeper, as his own passion raged, until with my name on his lips, we both went over the edge.

Sex? I had not had sex until that moment. Everything else had been a pale imitation of the act. That had been far more than lust. There had been a sense of belonging, of coming home, of forging a connection beyond time and space. That was more than great sex. It had been an affirmation that we belonged together, tonight and always.

Lee shifted us slightly, putting us on our sides, his body spooning mine. My heart still beat out a tattoo, my breathing, rapid and strained, but if there was a heaven, I'd just been there. I closed my eyes, ignoring the fact that I should go home. I'd just had the ride of my life. I couldn't wait for the next one.

His lips traced the side of my face, placing delicate kisses on the fevered flesh.

"I've wanted to do that from the moment I saw you, struggling to put on a brave front."

I giggled. "You saw me two days ago, and I was hardly struggling, although I was sad to see it all end."

He was quiet a moment. "That's what I meant. You were holding it all together, making people laugh … you're amazing, and I want you more than I've ever wanted anything."

"Then take me," I whispered. "I'm all yours." And I was.

"You're absolutely perfect," he whispered, before turning me onto my back once more and recreating the miracle he'd performed only a short while ago. "I can guarantee that tonight will never be enough to quench the need I have for you."

Bending his head, he captured my lips, eliminating the few rational thoughts trying to slip in, the ones that screamed at me to tell him the truth now, before it was too late.

Once more, like a sculptor creating the image he wanted to carve into the rock before him, his hands and lips moved along my body, studying me, memorizing every nuance of my body. As before, his fingers played my vagina as if it were a rare and unique instrument, given over to his expertise. Each thrust of his fingers made my body sing, pulling me closer and closer to the edge of the precipice once more. When I could barely stand the mounting pressure, he sheathed himself a second time and entered me, my body growing to accommodate his size and girth, Nature's magic to ensure the continuation of the species. Thrust after thrust pulled me closer to oblivion, and when I went over the edge, he followed.

We stayed entwined like that, two hearts beating as one until our breathing eased, and we slept.

* * *

The aroma of fresh brewed coffee filled my nostrils. I opened my eyes and stretched catlike, wincing at the soreness between my legs. Lee and I had made love at least twice more last night, and I felt absolutely wonderful today. Had I left him wanting more?

I had, but so had he. My hunger for the man was insatiable.

The bedroom door opened.

Lee, dressed in a hotel robe, his hair still wet from the shower, stepped into the room.

I smiled. "You should've waited for me," I teased. "I could use a shower, too."

"And here I thought you'd want a hot, bubbly bath."

He set the cup on the night table and kissed me. His breath was minty sweet while mine probably tasted like the bottom of a bird cage.

"Good morning. Was I wrong? Would you prefer a shower to a bath?"

I sat up, reached for the coffee, and sipped. It was just the way I liked it.

"How did you know how I take it?"

"You told me last night."

I didn't recall doing so, but we'd talked about so many things, like the bath.

I chuckled. "I told you lots of things."

"Yes, you did." He smirked. "Come on. The bath is ready and waiting for you. If you play your cards right, I just might wash your back."

I cocked my head, running my hand along the exposed skin at his throat.

"And my front?"

"Any part of you that you want." His eyes darkened with passion once more. He reached for my hand and pulled me up. "If you agree, after you finish soaking to your heart's content, we'll take a cab to your place. I left my car in a lot nearby. Then, I thought you could show me Venice Beach."

I grinned. "You're on."

By the time I got out of the bath, my fingers were wrinkled, and the floor was covered by towels to sop up the water we'd spilled when he'd joined me in the tub. It was a miracle we hadn't drowned.

The cab ride to my place was a short one, and while I dressed for the day, Lee left to collect his car. When he returned, I was ready, my sketch pad in my bag, and my body coated in sunscreen.

The day in Venice Beach was by far the best one ever. When he removed his shirt, I got a good look at his scars.

"What happened?" The question was out before I could stop it.

"I was in an accident as a child. There was a fire, and I was badly burned. It took a lot of skilled plastic surgeons to repair the damage."

I swallowed. "Does it hurt?"

"It did when it happened, but not now—at least not as longs as I don't sunburn it."

"I have something for that."

I removed the jar of cream from my bag and rubbed his back. We swam and then lounged in the shade on the blanket I'd brought. Mid-morning, I settled back against a rock and started drawing. I'd wanted to sketch him, but that seemed too intimate for now. Instead, I made several caricatures which I sold to pay for lunch.

We headed back to my place in the late afternoon deciding on take-out pizza and beer for dinner. While I knew I might be tempting fate, we watched *Pretty Woman* on one of the movie channels. When Stucky appeared and hit on Veronica the first time, I admitted that I'd secretly given that nickname to the Rayburn lawyer the night I'd met him.

He'd laughed. "You're a good judge of character. Having worked with the man a time or two, I agree."

Later that night, we explored one another again. It wasn't sex, it was love. Nothing that beautiful could simply be lust.

The next two months followed the same pattern. In the morning, he worked with the architects at the club. He'd asked me to sketch what I saw as the perfect, most functional bar. I'd even had a say in the new uniforms—black pants, black shirts, and silvery white bowties. Gender neutrality at its finest.

In the afternoons, we explored LA and the little towns along the coast. I drew, painted, and just lazed in his arms, more content than I'd ever expected. While he hadn't said the L word yet, the one that would require me to confess the truth, I knew he did—a woman just did. It was in the little gestures he made, like finding bluebonnets in LA.

I'd moved some of my clothing to his hotel suite. My bathroom had no tub, and there was no way we could shower together in my tiny box shower—he could hardly fit in it by himself.

Each night, we continued getting to know each other, to understand what brought us the greatest pleasure, and we always fell asleep satiated. There wasn't an inch of my body that he didn't know intimately, just as I knew his.

I was happier than I'd ever been, but as each day passed, the deadline approached, and I was no closer to getting my happily ever after.

As the dog days of summer went by, my joy and elation waned. I missed the ranch and the horses, but I also missed Texas. LA was fine, but it was crowded. I longed for open spaces and fresh air, free from smog and the endless sounds of humanity. As Amalia had put it, I had my cake and a fork to eat it with, but I still wasn't satisfied.

My emotions ran the gambit from ecstasy to misery. My conscience ate at me, with a reminder that a relationship built on a foundation of lies was sure to fail, and yet I couldn't reveal the truth. It was too soon, and while I was sure he loved me, I still needed proof—I needed that proposal.

Lee spent more and more time at the bar, seeing to last minute details and arranging for the entertainment. I did my part from home or his hotel room, ordering the beer, wine, and liquor we would need, setting up regular deliveries, and coordinating with the kitchen for the fruit and pickles required once we were back in business.

If I was alone, I would torment myself with the fact that I would soon be gone and someone else would have to take over behind the bar. If Lee was with me, I would delude myself that this fantasy could be real, that he could ask Cole Rayburn to stay on as the manager once the club was functional, and we could live out our lives just as we were doing now. The only time I felt truly safe was in his arms.

I refused to believe that anything, even the truth, could come between us. Together, we were invincible. I romanticized his elation when he realized who I was and what we could do with my money at our disposal. I pictured us setting up entertainment venues of our own in West Texas—dude ranches, riding academies, even our own rodeo circuit with a string of Texas-themed bars across the country. We could go international and take Texas to the world, but deep inside there was a voice warning me that everything could just as easily go wrong.

CHAPTER TWELVE

The end of August found me moodier than ever. I did my best to hide it from Lee who seemed to be dealing with issues of his own, but the last few days, there had been a desperation to our couplings, almost as if our bodies, if not our minds, knew our time was coming to an end.

The morning before the grand re-opening, Lee informed me that we would be going to the Casa Del Oro for dinner once more. He was nervous, and when I commented on it, he laughed it off, claiming it was simply a case of opening night jitters. I hoped it was more than that.

In keeping with the theme of revisiting our first date, I dressed as I had that night in my little black dress. I'd even managed to make a visit to the hairdresser and get my mani and pedi.

As the evening wore on, Lee seemed nervous, as if something supremely important weighed on him. I crossed my fingers and prayed he was about to grant my fondest wish, tell me he loved me, and beg me to marry him. In one of my crazed moments, I'd decided to compromise, give up being a vet, and follow him wherever Rayburn sent him. If a Japanese princess could give up her royal status and everything that went with it for love, I could give up a few measly billions. We didn't need Daddy's money. Money didn't buy happiness. It never had. We were happy just as we were, ordinary working people carving out a future for ourselves. If Daddy wasn't happy with my chosen path, then that was unfortunate, but absolutely nothing would keep me from marrying Lee. All he had to do was ask.

As before, the meal was superb, and just as we were finishing our wine, his cell phone rang. I didn't think I'd ever heard it ring before. He glanced at the screen, his brow creasing.

"I have to take this, Andie. Excuse me."

He stood and went outside. Through the window, I saw him arguing with whoever was at the other end of the line. Eventually, he came in again, his face a mask of misery.

"This isn't the way I expected tonight to end, honey, but something's come up that I have to deal with right away."

He signaled the waiter for the check. The man looked so worried that my heart went out to him. I didn't ask questions, just followed him out of the restaurant.

"Does it have to do with tomorrow night?"

He nodded.

"Then go and take care of it. I'll take a cab to my place. We can celebrate tomorrow."

He pulled me to him and kissed me with a desperation that surprised me. Fear ate at my gut. What could possibly be so bad?

He released my mouth and raised his head, leaning his brow against mine, his gaze filled with agony.

I wanted to ask what was wrong, but I stayed silent, frightened by an inner voice that screamed, *you don't want to know.*

"I hope so. I certainly hope so. I love you, Andie, I want you to know that. I've loved you from the very beginning. This wasn't the way I'd planned to say it, but—"

I put my hand up, one finger covering his lips, my heart overflowing with joy, blinking rapidly to keep the tears back.

"Stop. I love you, too. I have for a very long time, and while I'd like to prove it to you tonight, I sense you need to take care of whatever's tearing you apart first." I smiled weakly. "Unless you object, I'll take this cab and see you tomorrow at the club." I kissed him softly and opened the cab door. "Everything will work out."

"It has to," he whispered, the fear in his eyes almost palpable, "because if it doesn't, I don't know what I'll do."

He closed the cab door.

I gave the driver my address, looking back in time to see Lee get into a taxi of his own, the sudden tears blurring my vision.

Two questions tore at me. What could possibly have happened to cause him such anguish? How was that going to affect our future?

* * *

Late the following afternoon, after waiting endlessly for Lee's call, I took a cab to work. The club was still called The Pickleback, but it boasted a neon sign with the graphic I'd designed for it. My joy at seeing my old colleagues momentarily overran my disquiet. It was like a family reunion. Jess, Glenda, Luce, and Eugene were there, as was Tank. Two other servers had been hired to help out. They might only be part-time, but given the crowd already there by five, we were going to need them tonight.

Opening night entertainment featured Raffey as the headliner, a couple of other comedians I'd seen on television, and two singers, one of which had done well on American Idol. There was an MC to introduce the acts—Lee had offered to let me do it, but I'd said no. It would probably be hard enough to replace me when the time came for me to go, and if he turned down my offer—something I'd had nightmares about the previous night—well, enough said. Lou was back as DJ with a fancy booth to himself, and a dance floor had been added.

While I was a basket of nerves, seeing the bar exactly as I'd envisioned it was gratifying. It was a bartender's dream, everything right at my fingertips. The only thing spoiling the moment was Lee's continued absence. The fact that he wasn't here ate at me. Something was wrong. Something was very, very wrong. I'd called his cell phone, and the call had gone directly to voice mail. Sadly, I had no time to ponder the problem. As the saying went, the show must go on. The place was crazy busy, and after a two-month hiatus, I wasn't quite up to my usual speed.

By eleven o'clock, Lee was still a no-show, the bar was swinging, with the patrons happy and soaking up alcohol like sponges, but I was absolutely miserable. I kept telling myself that there had to be a logical explanation for his absence, but the later it got, the harder it was to believe it.

I had my back to the crowd, mixing a Bloody Mary, trying to stay focused on the task at hand and not dreaming up one horrible scenario after another. My stomach had been wonky all day, and the smell of the tomato juice and vodka weren't helping. Had I eaten since last night? I couldn't recall.

"Well, I'll be damned. The insufferable little weasel was right. He said he'd found you. I knew you and your sisters were up to something, but this…" She shook her head. "Best two hundred and fifty grand I've ever spent."

My head snapped up. My eyes fixed on the mirror in front of me the way a driver focuses on the rearview mirror of the vehicle he's driving. The air vanished from the room. Standing at the bar, dripping in sequins and diamonds, was the one woman I'd hoped never to see again.

"Hello, Andressa. Surprised to see me? You really shouldn't be. People have been looking for you for months. I see you put your father's money to good use. You're the spitting image of your mother." She chuckled bitterly. "Ugly duckling Andressa Myers transformed into Andie Harper, beautiful swan and a bartender of all things. Your father's going to be beside himself. I can't wait to see his face when he sees the papers in the morning."

I gasped. It wasn't Becki's words that stunned me. It was the look of compassion on the face of the man who'd just entered the bar, the man I loved. The man I thought loved me.

My gaze met his in the mirror, and slowly things fell into place. There was no stunned surprise on his face, no shock, nothing but an emotion I labeled regret. There it was. The ugly truth in all its despicable colors. He'd known my true identity all along. He hadn't wanted me. He'd wanted the Myers billions. His plan had almost succeeded. I'd fallen in love with him, ready to say yes when he asked me to marry him, and once I did, all Daddy's money would drop into his lap. God, what a fool I was and what a fantastic actor he was. And his performance in bed? The look on his face last night when he'd confessed his love? Oscar-worthy.

So, what had happened? Why hadn't he followed through with his plan? Whoever had called him last night must've known something was up, because if his backing down from the proposal hadn't been a case of cold feet, nothing was. Had he gotten wind of this impending disaster? Whoever had said when it's too good to be true, it probably is, must've had this scenario in mind. He'd made a fool of me.

No, he didn't. You did that all by yourself.

My imaginary rose-colored glasses lay smashed at my feet. There was no bigger fool than the person who believed they could ignore the reality of who and what they were. I could never be just an ordinary person. Sooner or later, someone would see behind the mask, and I would be revealed. I was that fool. I'd been so smart, so savvy with my grand plan to find someone to love me for me, someone whose love came without a price tag attached to it. What a joke. I should've known it was impossible. All I'd bought was shame and pain. Sure, I'd had mind-blowing sex, but it had come at too high a price. Becki was right. Daddy would be furious, and he would have every right to be. I'd have no choice but to marry the first man he threw at me. Soiled goods. My shame and stupidity out there for all the world to see.

Now that the moment of truth had arrived, I was strangely calm. It was over, more dramatically than I expected, but all performances eventually ended. It was time for my final bow.

I turned to face the woman who'd just hoisted me on my own petard. Maybe I should thank her for saving me from a gold digger. Daddy would probably reward her with a diamond big enough to choke a horse. I refused to look at Lee. I had nothing to say to him. The look on his face had said it all.

"Hello, Becki, not that I'm happy to see you, but you didn't expect me to be, did you?"

The bright white of flash photography filled the semi-darkness of the bar. There was no point in denying it. The slew of reporters with her were snapping their cameras so quickly that I had flashbulb burn. Within minutes, my picture would be all over the Internet and headed for the cover of every damn magazine and newspaper in the country. Once more, I was Andressa Myers, billionaire heiress, a celebrity, and the last thing I ever wanted to be.

Becki had even supplied the perfect headline. Ugly Duckling Heiress Turns into Beautiful Swan Bartender. The media would eat the story up, and what they couldn't find, they would make up, just as they always had.

Jess, who'd been standing by the bar when Becki had dropped her bomb, was the first to recover, if you could consider her shock and awe recovery.

"What's going on, Andie. Who are these people?" She turned to the photographer who'd just taken her picture. "If that thing flashes in my face one more time, the next picture it's going to take will be of your alimentary canal when I shove it down your throat." She turned back to me. "So? What is all this, and who the hell is Andressa Myers?"

Her voice carried across the suddenly quiet room. Lou, having noted the commotion at the bar, had stopped the music. Low voices filled the area, the sound strangely similar to that of a swarm of angry bees getting ready to attack.

Before I could answer, Fred, one of the regulars who'd sat at my bar for months, slammed his fist on the counter and shook his head.

"Son of a bitch! She is. She's the missing heiress we've been searching for this past year. Talk about a publicity stunt. Rayburn sure as hell knows how to put a spot on the map. She's the one who had sunstroke and then vanished. I've been working that case for months, and she's been right here under my nose the entire time." He turned to me, narrowing his eyes. "I should've seen it. You look just like your mother, and I have a dozen pictures of her in the file I put together. I knew everything about you—or rather I thought I did. Strange, you were never a beauty, a little cute when you smiled and relaxed, but … Plastic surgery? The boob job I can see, but you rearranged your whole damn face. I can't imagine hating myself enough to erase myself like that. Did you enjoy your time among the peasants, my lady? I sure as hell didn't expect to find a billionaire heiress slinging beer in East LA. I guess the joke was on me and the rest of the schmucks working here."

Jess paled. "Is it true? Is this just a publicity stunt? Are you really someone else?"

There was no point in denying it. I was frozen in place, unable to escape, unable to do anything but watch and play my part for the last time.

"Yes, no, and yes." I uttered my line, well aware that it created more pain and sorrow.

Surprise turned to anger. "And you changed your face? I thought you were my friend, Andie. I shared everything with you, and what did you share in return? A big freaking lie. Are you even from Texas?"

Becki laughed. "That's one thing she didn't lie about, but everything else about her is fake." She threw an old tabloid on the table, one with what was probably the worst photograph ever taken of me.

Jess picked it up.

"There she is before she spent a ton of her father's money to make her look beautiful instead of the freak she was, and even then, she didn't know enough to get a bust large enough to brag about," she snarled. "You're pathetic."

"That's enough, Mrs. Myers," Lee stated, anger vibrating in his voice as he moved closer to the bar. "This is a comedy club, and you aren't on tonight's schedule. I suggest you take your trained monkeys and leave."

Becki turned on him with the speed of an attacking viper, her eyes ablaze, the apples of her cheeks redder than they should be.

"I don't know who the hell you think you are, but you're messing with the wrong woman. Do you know who I am?"

His eyes narrowed. "All too well. I know precisely who you are. You're a bad-mannered, rich bitch who's no different tonight than when I met you at Andressa's birthday party."

Recognition dawned in her step-mother's eyes, and she burst out laughing.

"Oh my God. The waiter. This just gets better and better. I knew you two were up to something that night, but I never expected you to stoop so low, Andressa, as to try to fit in and become one of them. Was the plastic surgery his suggestion? Most likely it was, or you would've done something about your looks years ago. How the mighty have fallen." She turned to the reporters. "Got enough, guys?"

Choruses of, "Oh yeah," answered her.

Somehow, I found my tongue. "Becki, I need to know. How did your man find me?"

She chuckled. "The detective? He couldn't find his ass if he needed to wipe it, but you drew him right to you. He was in Venice Beach last month with his niece. You sketched a picture of a pelican for her. You signed it with the letter A, the same way you do everything you draw. Something about the way you made that letter seemed familiar to him. When he got home, he sifted through his research and found copies of the sketches you'd won the art competition with years ago, one of them of a similar bird, but it was the signature that cinched it. He took the sketches to a graphologist who told him they'd been made by the same person. Vanity's a sin, Andressa, and it brought about your ruin. Had you not signed that sketch, he would probably still be searching for you. It'll take a lot of ten-dollar drawings to support you without your father's money, because I can't see him ever forgiving you for what you've done. Maybe you should try turning—"

Lee stood within inches of her. "I would think very hard before finishing that sentence," he warned.

"Since when does a glorified waiter get to tell me what to do or say? I got you fired that night, and I'll do it again. As to her, you were wasting your time. You wouldn't have gotten any money, you know. Andressa's wealth is in a trust fund under her father's control, and he sure as hell wouldn't have turned it over to you. It would've taken a miracle for that to happen."

Or a grandson.

I grabbed the counter. All the sex we'd had … not even the best method of birth control was foolproof, and all we'd used had been prophylactics. One pinhole. It only took one pinhole in a condom for one lucky little swimmer to win the sweepstakes.

"Hey, buddy," one of the reporters called. "What's your name so I can get it right in the article."

Lee turned to me, his face mirroring his chagrin. "It's Leland James Cole Rayburn. Do I have to spell it out for you?"

He didn't. I could read between the lines. I'd been conned. My father had set me up. The Freaky Four had been nothing more than a distraction. This man had been his choice, and he'd set me up to prove that he knew what I wanted even when I didn't. Daddy always got his way.

The shock on Becki's face was genuine. Before I could lash out at her, the room began to spin, the faces and decorations around me melting like Dali's watches. The room spun faster and faster as I slipped into a pit of darkness.

* * *

When I came to, I lay on the couch in Lee's darkened office. Bit by bit, like pieces of a puzzle, it all came back to me—Becki, Lee, and the ultimate betrayal. Leland James Cole Rayburn, the man my father had picked to win the Myers Marriage Sweepstakes, the man who'd made a fool of me.

Why had he been at my birthday party in disguise? Had that all been part of my father's sick little game? Or had he come to check out the material for himself before committing to anything? What had he said? He liked to do his own research. Had he decided I would do? No doubt, he'd found me lacking, but then I'd had the plastic surgery. It must've been quite the surprise to find me tending bar in his newly acquired club.

When had he recognized me? How had he recognized me? Had it been my perfume? My laughter? He must've gotten a hell of a kick from it. That was why he'd never said anything about my breast implants. He knew exactly why they were there.

My head pounded with all the unanswerable questions running through my mind. The sound of music filtering through the wall pointed to the fact that with or without me, despite that momentary hiccup, the show had gone on.

I groaned and sat up. What a fool I was. I needed to get out of here and go somewhere to figure out my next step.

"Take it easy, Andie. The paramedics are on their way."

Paramedics were the last people I wanted to see, especially if I was pregnant. I stood, my fight or flight instinct fully engaged in flight mode.

"Jess, everything you heard was true, but it's not what you think. It was never meant to be a publicity stunt, at least not on my part, although thanks to my step-mother … I never intended to hurt anyone. I'll explain it all one day, but I have to get out of here. I can't face any of them now. Is your car out back?"

"It is, but do you think you should drive?" The concern on her face shook me more than I thought it would.

"I'm fine. I skipped lunch because I was worried about—" Obviously, he was just fine. "About tonight." I sighed. "I can't stay here now. I'll take your car to my place and leave your keys with my landlady. I know someone who's close to a casting agent. I guarantee he'll get you a decent part. Call it my going away present. It's the least I can do for a friend, and I did consider you a friend."

"You don't have to do that, Andie." She came over to me. "I don't know why you did what you did, and I'm sorry I said what I did. Here are the keys. Go out the back way. It's parked right next to the door. What do you want me to tell Mr. Rayburn—and wasn't that a surprise?"

My only consolation was that she and the rest of the staff hadn't known Lee and I were a couple, although she might've figured it our from Becki's comments.

"Nothing. Tell him that you went to the bathroom, and when you came back, I was gone."

With that I hugged her and escaped out the back door.

Quickly unlocking the car, I climbed inside, pulled out my cell phone, and called Phil, the UBER driver I used.

"Hey, Phil, it's Andie.'

"Hi, Andie. I didn't expect to hear from you so soon. I drove by there a little while ago. The place was hopping. Want me to pick you up later?"

I swallowed, fighting to keep my voice level.

"Actually, there's an emergency back home, and I need to get to the airport. Can you meet me at my place in twenty minutes?"

"Sure thing. I don't have a pickup for an hour."

"Thanks."

As soon as I got to my place, I parked the car and hurried up to my apartment. Unlocking my door, I entered, grabbed my suitcase, and tossed my essentials into it. A lot of my stuff was in Lee's—no, Cole's—hotel room. I would have to learn to live without it. I took the brown wig I'd bought thinking I might use it as a disguise at Halloween and shoved it in my purse along with my passport which was useless thanks to my surgery, my bank cards, and the cash I'd stashed in the freezer.

I wrote a quick note to Mrs. Richards, thanking her, telling her I no longer needed the apartment, that she was welcome to everything in it, and explaining about Jess's car keys. I left my apartment, locking the door behind me, and dropping all the keys and the note in her mailbox.

When Phil arrived, I was waiting for him. I had him take me to LAX, and paid him double the fee, wishing him and his wife well.

At the airport, I paid cash for a ticket to Anchorage, Alaska, the only flight leaving within the hour, went into the bathroom, changed out of my bartender uniform, put on jeans and an old sweatshirt, and then covered my hair with the brown wig. As soon as my transformation was complete, I tossed the uniform in the trash and left the airport, grabbing a bus back into the city. Eventually, I made my way to Long Beach. By morning, I was waiting to board a flight to Catalina.

* * *

Gazing out at the rain, I let the melancholy enfold me. Since I'd arrived at Shangri-la three days ago, I'd done nothing but cry, sleep, and stare out the window.

When I'd left LA, I'd done a good job of covering my tracks, but I doubted anyone was looking for me. By now, Daddy would know I'd defied him, and my new face would be all over. I wouldn't be able to walk down a street for months without the paparazzi hounding me. The only choice I had was to go back to Quaternity—if Daddy would let me. If not, I had access to a small trust left by my mother. I would lay low here a while longer and then find a hiding place in the backwoods. What I would do after that was as yet a mystery.

The only one who might think to look here would be Amalia. Despite what Becki had said, I refused to believe my sisters could've been a part of this deception. They loved me. They'd tried to help me.

If any thing good did come from the disaster, it would be the fact that The Pickleback was an unmitigated success. I'd watched some of the news coverage. The entertainment wouldn't be its only drawing card. People would be going in there just to be *where* it had all happened.

Discovering the missing heiress, new face and all, had been a tempest in a teapot, compared to the unveiling of the identity of Rayburn Enterprises' CEO. Why had he done it? He could've left his name as Lee James and been done with it. No one would've been any wiser. What had he hoped to gain by revealing his identity? Other than letting me know what an absolute, gullible idiot I'd been.

I reached for the sketch pad and stared at the drawing I'd made. I'd recalled Lee staring out at the ocean and had drawn him in profile. I still didn't know what I was going to do. I loved the man, dang it, loved him as much as I had on the evening that I'd admitted it outside the restaurant. I missed him more than I'd missed anyone since Mama had died, but he'd hurt me. He'd hurt me badly, and I wasn't sure I could get beyond that.

He'd claimed to love me, but how could I believe that when everything he'd said had been a lie? I chose to ignore my own untruths. They had nothing to do with *his* deception. Besides, he'd known who I was, so my keeping my identity from him was a moot point.

Someone knocked on the cabin door. Unlike my first visit here when I was a surgical patient, I was now housed in a beautiful three-room cabin. Anything I wanted was available with a simple call to the concierge. At the moment, breakfast sat on a tray at the far side of the room. The smell of it was enough to turn my stomach. I hadn't had much of an appetite since arriving.

That first morning, when Ingrid had opened the door, I'd burst into tears. After listening to my tale of woe, she'd shown me to the cabin, and I'd slept the rest of the day. Yesterday, Will had come over and given me an extremely thorough physical, but while I wasn't feverish, I just felt blah. No doubt the emotional toil was to blame, but how long could I go on like this?

CHAPTER THIRTEEN

I stood, my bloated stomach making my jeans too tight for comfort. Odd how I'd hardly eaten for days and yet suddenly felt fat and out of sorts. It looked as though my body, like everything else in my life, had decided to betray me, those twenty pounds of fat cells I'd shed, slowly finding their way home. I'd heard depression could cause all kinds of physical issues, but this was ridiculous.

"Come in," I called, expecting the concierge to be there to collect the tray.

Will stepped into the room, eyed the uneaten breakfast tray, and smirked.

"Food not to your liking this morning?"

I shook my head. "No. It's fine. I'm just not hungry. It must be the weather. I seem to be retaining water. Could be my period…"

He nodded. "Not surprising. You've had a lousy seventy-two hours. Tell me, other than the queasy stomach, bloating, lack of appetite, and lethargy, how do you feel?"

I glanced at the sketch. Lonely. I was lonely.

"Sad, I guess. Disappointed, let down, hurt," I finished.

"Your emotions are going to be all over the place for the next few weeks, and while you'll have to work those out for yourself, I'll start you on vitamins and a tonic, and see you get a lighter breakfast tomorrow with mint tea to start the day. I'm afraid you'll only be allowed one cup of coffee a day, and that'll be low test, but you'll be fine."

I frowned, my mouth going dry. I'd suspected a virus or something, but…

"I'm sick?"

I immediately thought of the potential organ damage mentioned as a consequence of my heatstroke. What was it? Heart? Liver? Kidneys?

He laughed. "I wouldn't say you're sick, Andie, although you may have to take things a bit more slowly for the next few months. You're pregnant."

My eyes threatened to leave their sockets. Sure, the idea had crossed my mind when I'd imagined Lee had been after my father's money, but I hadn't thought of it again. I was pregnant. I was going to have a baby—Cole Rayburn's baby. What in God's name was I going to do?

I swallowed. "You're sure?"

"Absolutely. Your hCG levels are high. When was your last period?"

I'd never been particularly regular, but I realized that I hadn't had a period since I'd started having sex with Lee—Cole—it was all so confusing.

"I'm not as regular as most women, but I haven't had one since the end of June."

"Then that puts you at a maximum of ten weeks, which fits with what I saw when I examined you. Your due date should be around the beginning of April, give or take a week." He rubbed his chin. "You're already experiencing some of the physical changes. What you called bloating probably isn't, and that queasy stomach you mentioned yesterday is most likely morning sickness. You shouldn't have an issue breastfeeding since the incision is under the fold, but that's up to you. I know that this child isn't what you wanted, and you need time to think about everything. The situation isn't perfect, but…" He shrugged and stood.

"Have you told anyone else," I whispered.

He shook his head, his face a mask of compassion. "No, Andie. You're my patient. I won't even tell Ingrid without your permission, although I'm sure she'll be thrilled. What happens next is your decision, not anyone else's." He reached for the tray. "I'll have Bruno bring you some dry toast and mint tea."

As soon as he left, I sagged against the couch and burst into tears. Pregnant. It looked as if fate would have the last laugh after all.

"Won't Daddy be happy," I groaned before dissolving into a fresh round of tears.

I'd just pulled myself together again, when someone knocked on the door once more.

"Come in," I called, not having the energy to even stand.

Bruno pushed the door open, balancing the tray in one hand. He wasn't alone. Amalia stood on the doorstep.

"Andie, can I come in?"

I nodded. No reason why she shouldn't. None of this mess was her fault.

Bruno entered and set the tray on the coffee table in front of the couch.

I thanked him, and he left, closing the door behind him.

Amalia stood there just inside the doorway, waiting.

"Sit."

I indicated the chair Will had vacated earlier after he'd delivered the monumental news that had further shaken my world.

Amalia sighed and sat, her eyes filled with sorrow.

"Andie, we need to talk."

I shrugged. "I suppose we should. Are you here to give me more bad news? Becki made it plain that Daddy would be furious. By the way, when did you realize I'd run here?"

"That woman was right about one thing. Daddy is furious, but he isn't mad at you. He's divorcing her. She stepped over the line again. He'd warned her the night you collapsed. Maria packed up everything she owned and had it delivered to the penthouse in Dallas, the apartment that's now hers under the pre-nup."

"You're serious?" That at least was good news.

"Yes, but I think she'd outlived her usefulness months ago. She flew home from Singapore because the ship made her seasick. He didn't come back with her." Amalia exhaled heavily. "As for

332

knowing where you were, it wasn't a guess. We've known where you were every step of the way. Did you honestly think Daddy would've agreed to any of this if he hadn't been able to keep track of you?"

"Of course not," I spat, angry at myself for not realizing it sooner. "What did he do? Have the doctor implant a tracker under my skin while I was in that induced coma?"

"No, but I'm sure if he'd thought of it, he might have." She chuckled. "It's in the heel of your boots. You love those things. You never go anywhere without them."

I laughed. So simple and so true. Once more my naivety was brought home to me.

Did you know Lee was Cole Rayburn?" I challenged. I'd waxed poetic about the man the last two months.

Amalia nodded. "I did, but before you get angry, it isn't what you think. I recognized him at your birthday party because I'd met him a few months earlier when I'd accompanied Dan to New York to discuss a potential merger. I didn't know what he was doing there, other than the fact he had a history of checking out business matters for himself. That was the first time Quaternity had used Rayburn Catering. I assumed he was making sure his people got everything right. Dan knew he was there, but since we had no idea why, we decided to let the game play out. You looked great that night— not that you were ever a freak like Becki claimed. You know me and secrets. Well, I had to tell someone, so I mentioned it to the twins. Aileen thought he was quite handsome. We saw him bring you the chair and snub the prince, so we decided to help you both find one another. We weren't sure how we'd bring you together, but we were working out the details when you collapsed. After that, everything just fell into place. To be fair, we had planned to convince Daddy to let you have the surgery since it meant so much to you."

Tears burned my eyes as her words sunk in. She'd not only known who he was, she'd been part of the deception.

"So, it was all a set up, and you were in on it." The pain of betrayal tore at me once more. I was too hurt to be angry. "This was all part of Daddy's plan to get what he wanted, regardless of what it did to me. Was any of it ... was any of it real?"

"God, Andie, don't even think that way. We were trying to help you, trying to give you the dream you wanted. It wasn't all bad, was it? You got to be an ordinary person for a little while. You knew it couldn't last forever. Cole's name might've come up as a potential husband for you because Daddy and Leland Rayburn were old friends, and he wanted to unite the families as well as the companies, but no one was trying to hurt you, trying to force you to do something you didn't want to do. I told you. The choice was always yours. It still is. Cole Rayburn has stayed out of the limelight all those years for the same reason you did. He wanted to live a normal life, the kind of life he'd had in Pennsylvania, the kind of life he lost when his uncle died, but that's his story to tell." She stood and came to sit beside me, reaching for my hand.

"Honey, you were so determined to find someone you could love on your own that I was sure you'd get your back up and walk away even if the perfect man presented himself. I'll give Daddy credit for one thing. He went out of his way to find the four most unsuitable men he could."

I brushed away a tear. "He certainly did but letting them think I might marry one of them was rather mean."

She laughed. "Maybe, on the surface, but they all got something out of it. Lincoln Ford and Nataly Raynes have gone into partnership to produce energy pellets made from dung that can be used to replace coal in power plants. If it works out, it'll make them both quite rich. Mom has arranged an Arctic expedition for Lyle and Lettie, and Jackson won his seat in congress thanks to Daddy's generous donation to his campaign. As for Prince Leopold, it seems he's been involved in one too many attempts to overthrow his government and is on the run once more, looking for someone to sooth his lack of success." She shook her head. "I don't get it. Why are you torturing yourself like this? You were already half in love with the man when you thought he was a waiter who'd taken the time the night of your birthday to be nice to you and rub your feet. Considering he did, the odds were he was just as fascinated by you. Over the past few weeks, I heard the happiness in your voice when you talked about him. You love him, I know you do. It seems you both wanted the same thing, even if you did both go about it ass-backwards. You wanted someone to fall in love with you for yourself and not your bank account. Is it so hard to believe he may have wanted the same thing? You have to let him explain. You've always prided yourself on being openminded. So, what are you going to do now?"

I burst into tears once more. Dang hormones.

"I don't know, Amalia. I just don't know.

* * *

Two weeks later, knowing I couldn't hide at Shangri-la forever, I'd returned to the ranch. It was late afternoon, and I sat in the shade on the patio. As much as Daddy had wanted to celebrate my birthday, I'd refused. I wasn't in the mood to party. I might never be in that mood again.

I'd dug out a few of my items of clothing I'd worn twenty pounds ago, including a blouson swimsuit, but I hadn't told anyone about the baby. I had an appointment with an obstetrician in Lubbock next week. Will had already sent him my files, and he would take over my pre-natal care. I was going to keep the baby, that was a given, but before I told Daddy and the others, I owed it to Lee to tell him the truth. It was his child, a potential heir to his kingdom as well as mine.

I'd gone back to looking after the animals, but I intended to keep Ken French, the vet who'd been looking after the ranch, as my assistant. While I still rode, I limited my rides to short, easy lopes.

I reached for the glass of cranberry juice on the table beside me, a shadow falling over me as I did.

"Hello, Andie."

I jerked, spilling some of the juice as I put the glass back on the table.

Glancing behind me, I took in the man I loved. My heart leapt for joy, while my brain screamed, *don't go there.*

He wore a white golf shirt and gray pants. He was clean-shaven, his hair recently cut and styled, but his eyes were shadowed as if he hadn't slept in weeks.

Given the way the paparazzi dogged his every step, he probably hadn't. I didn't know what he expected from me. Anger? Fury? Did he think I would throw myself into his arms and beg him to hold me again? It wasn't going to happen—at least not until we'd laid all our cards on the table.

"Hello, Lee, or should I say Cole." My voice caught in my throat.

"Lee is fine. It's what my mother always called me, and I did say you could call me whatever you liked."

I nodded. "Why are you here, Lee?" I wasn't going to make this easy on him.

He kept his distance, his shadowed eyes dark with emotion, his brow deeply furrowed.

"Because I've missed you, Andie. Not a second has passed since that night when I haven't craved you in my arms. Your step-mother was lucky to walk out of that club alive." He ran his hand through his hair. "When you collapsed … and then disappeared … I knew I had to give you time to get over your anger, but I can't go another day without you in my life. I know I should've been honest with you and told you I recognized you that night at The Pickleback, but that would've meant telling you who I was, and I wasn't ready for that."

"Why?"

"Pride … an overabundance of it, and fear. May I?" He indicated the chair across from me.

I nodded.

He sat, leaned forward, and laced his fingers in his lap.

"I was fourteen when my parents were killed in a plane crash. I was badly burned—you've seen my back—and not expected to live, but I've always been a fighter. My father was the younger son, an architect. He'd never expected to take over the company and neither did I. When I got out of the hospital, I went to live with my grandparents on their farm—not a ranch—in Pennsylvania. Granddad kept in touch, made sure I had everything I needed, but after seeing what the Press did to injured celebrities, he gave me the greatest gift of all, anonymity—what you got as Andie Harper. Their surname was James, and I chose to use the first part of my name only. So, Cole Rayburn disappeared from the media. It worked for me. When COVID killed my uncle, since he had no heirs, my grandfather asked me to take on the leadership role instead of the position I held in the finance department. I agreed, but with conditions, one of them being that Lee James could still do what I'd been doing, setting up new ventures, and Cole Rayburn would keep a low profile. He agreed.

It seemed to be working until a year ago when he told me that he wanted to see me married before he died and that he had the perfect girl for me. She was a veterinarian, smart, a little shy and self-conscious because she looked like her father but had a good heart. I would be the last person to ever judge another because of physical beauty. It took me years to be able to take off my shirt in public."

I nodded, sympathizing with him despite trying to maintain my anger.

"Go on." It was the only olive branch I offered.

"My first instinct was to say no, but the disappointment in his eyes made me reconsider, but like you, I've always been wary of the motives of those around me. He wanted something more from Quaternity than just a granddaughter-in-law. Please remember, I hadn't seen a lot of him growing up since he'd been consumed growing the business. At any rate, I met with your sister, Amalia, and her husband, Dan, to discuss a proposed merger to build a hotel outside of Lubbock. Your father invited me to your birthday party, and I offered to have

Rayburn Catering look after the party. Then, a couple of days before, I sent my regrets. The day of the party, I joined the staff. Andie, I don't know why you thought you were ugly, but I understand wanting to feel as though you fit in, but your eyes, those clear, dark blue pools filled with sorrow and fear, anger and determination drew me. The way you talked about it all, accepting to sacrifice yourself because you saw no easy way out … I knew you were someone I could love and respect. When I called on Monday to plan to come out to the ranch again and learned about your heatstroke, I thought I'd lost you before even having a chance with you. Do you know that I sat by your bedside with your father for two nights, waiting to hear that you were going to be okay? That was when we concocted this whole scheme, and of all the mistakes I've made in my life, that was by far the worst. I'm sorry I agreed to it, but Amalia was so sure that you'd get your dander up if I showed up and announced who I was before you got a chance to know me. I should've just come right out and told you the truth, but I was scared. When Amalia told me you recognized me and didn't say anything to me either, that you were obsessed about someone loving Andie Harper not Andressa Myers, I could empathize with that."

"I wanted to be loved for me, not Daddy's money," I defended my actions, which suddenly seemed silly.

He chuckled, confirming my thought. "Since I happen to have more money than he does, I think that's a moot point."

"Why did you lie about a problem concerning opening night when you left me at the restaurant? Did you know Becki planned to expose me?"

"No. If I had, believe me, I would've made sure to stop her in her tracks. I didn't lie. Chef Peters had ordered new grills for the kitchen and when they arrived that afternoon, no one noticed that the gas nozzles were in the wrong place until the men went to hook them us. The suppliers had sent the wrong stoves, and I had to scramble to find some. Temperamental chefs with the wrong equipment aren't good for business, but that wasn't why I was upset. I'd planned to tell you that I loved you—which I did—explain who I really was, and then after we went back to the hotel, I planned to ask you to marry me. I even had this with me. I'd picked it up from the jeweler that morning." He pulled a ring box out of his pocket but didn't open it. "The doorstep of a restaurant didn't seem to be the place for that, so since you wanted me to get if fixed and that we'd continue celebrating tomorrow, I took you at your word. I was up all night, driving to Las Vegas to get some of the grills we had in storage there and then arranging to get them hooked up. By the time, I got to bed, it was three in the afternoon. I only expected to sleep for a couple of hours. When I woke up, it was ten. I dressed and got there as fast as I could, just in time to see your step-mother perform. The look on your face … I blurted out my identity, not for the world to know but for you to know she was wrong about everything. I wasn't after your money. All I wanted was you."

Tears rolled down my cheeks.

"Andie, please tell me I still have a chance. Please tell me you'll forgive me. The night I made love to you, I told you that I'd wanted to ever since I first saw you, a year ago today, not a couple of nights earlier." He opened the ring box, revealing a beautiful marquise-cut sapphire surrounded by diamonds on a platinum band.

I stared at the gorgeous ring. It would match Mama's sapphires beautifully, completing the set.

"Say something," he pleaded. "Yell at me. Rant, rave, scream, but please don't sit there silently crying."

I swallowed and swiped at my tears."

"Just shut up and kiss me."

He needed no further prompting.

The kiss was more than a kiss. It was a cleansing of all the pain and misery I'd suffered. His lips fed from me as if I were the only source of life he had. I put all of my love into my response.

When we eventually came up for air, he smiled at me, the love in his eyes unmistakable.

"I take it that's a yes?"

He slipped the ring onto my finger. It was a perfect fit, but I still had news of my own to deliver.

"When did you want to get married?"

"If I thought your father and my grandfather would allow it, I'd take you to Vegas and do it tonight, but I doubt either would agree to that."

I giggled, filled with more joy than I would've thought possible.

"And neither would my sisters, but it's going to have to be soon. Please tell me you don't have shares in the company that produces the condoms you used."

He frowned. "I don't think so. Why would you—" His eyes grew wide, and his jaw dropped. "Are you saying what I think you are?"

I nodded. "We're going to be parents."

His face filled with joy. He jumped up and picked me up off the chair and swung me around.

"This is perfect, Andie, absolutely perfect."

I grinned. "Not quite. Perfect would've been having this happen next year, but it's good and sometimes good is just what you need."

His lips fastened on mine once more, erasing all the pain, anguish and doubts I'd had. The future was what we would make of it. Boy or girl didn't really matter. The child would be loved. Lee was right. Everything was perfect.

A Note From The Author

Thank you for taking the time to read Love at The Pickleback. I hope you enjoyed reading it as much as I enjoyed writing it. In life, we sometimes have to take a risk or take a stand and fight for what we believe. We may not always win, but we're guaranteed to lose every time we don't try. Things may not always be perfect, but they can be good, and often good enough is all you need.

If you enjoyed the book, please feel free to leave a review for it. Word of Mouth is the best kind of advertising.

Take care and stay safe,

Susanne

ABOUT THE AUTHOR

Susanne Matthews was born and raised in Eastern Ontario, Canada. She is of French-Canadian descent. She's always been an avid reader of all types of books, but with a penchant for happily ever after romances. A retired educator, Susanne spends her time writing and creating adventures for her readers. She loves the ins and outs of romance, and the complex journey it takes to get from the first word to the last period of a novel. As she writes, her characters take on a life of their own, and she shares their fears and agonies on the road to self-discovery and love.

Website: http://www.mhsusannematthews.ca/
Blog: https://aroundthedream.blog/
Facebook: https://www.facebook.com/SLMauthor
Author Amazon:
https://www.amazon.com/Susanne-Matthews/e/B00DJCKRP4
Goodreads:
https://www.goodreads.com/author/show/7009276.Susanne_Matthews
Twitter: @jandsmatt

Other Books From This Author

Romantic Suspense and Thrillers

The Harvester Files

The White Carnation, Book One

The White Lily, Book Two

The White Iris Book Three

The White Dahlia Book Four

Vengeance Is Mine

On His Watch, Book One

Fire Angel, Book Two

In Plain Sight, Book Three

No Good Deed, Book Four

Secrets and Lies Book Five

Protecting the Innocent

Sworn to Protect, Book 1

Guarding her Heart, Book 2

Other Suspense Novels

Desert Deception

Prove It! (Young Adult Suspense)

Paranormal

Mystic Adventures Series

Echoes of the Past(With Native American elements))

Hello Again (With Native American elements)

Atonement

Timeless Love Series

Beneath the Ashes

The Punishers

The Tigress

The Guardian

Historical Romances

The Captain's Promise

The Price of Honor, Canadiana Series, Book One

The Price of Courage Canadiana Series, Book Two

Twist of Fate, The Golden Legacy

Contemporary Romance:

All For Love Series:

Just for the Weekend

Forever and Always

Wedding Bell Blues

The Blue Dragon

Same Time Next Year

Royal Flush

The Regal Rose

Trouble with Eden

<u>Finding Melinda</u>

Cocktails for You Series

<u>Tequila Sunrise</u>

<u>Champagne Cocktail</u>

<u>Buck's Fizz</u>

<u>The Tipsy Pig</u>

<u>Make Mine a Manhattan</u>

<u>Emerald Glow</u>

<u>Sea Breeze</u>

<u>It's a Match</u>

<u>Noelle's Gambit</u>

Winter Weddings Series

<u>Holiday Magic</u>

<u>The Perfect Choice</u>

<u>Come Home for Christmas</u>

<u>Forever in my Heart</u>

Other Holiday Romances

<u>His Christmas Family</u> (Christmas)

<u>Murder & Mistletoe</u> (Holiday Suspense Romance)

Made in United States
North Haven, CT
06 June 2025